A Series of Textbooks of **Chinese U See**

象形卡通系列教科書

Body & Related Words

自體及相關的字

起步版 (Initial Edition)

3

Min Guo
郭敏

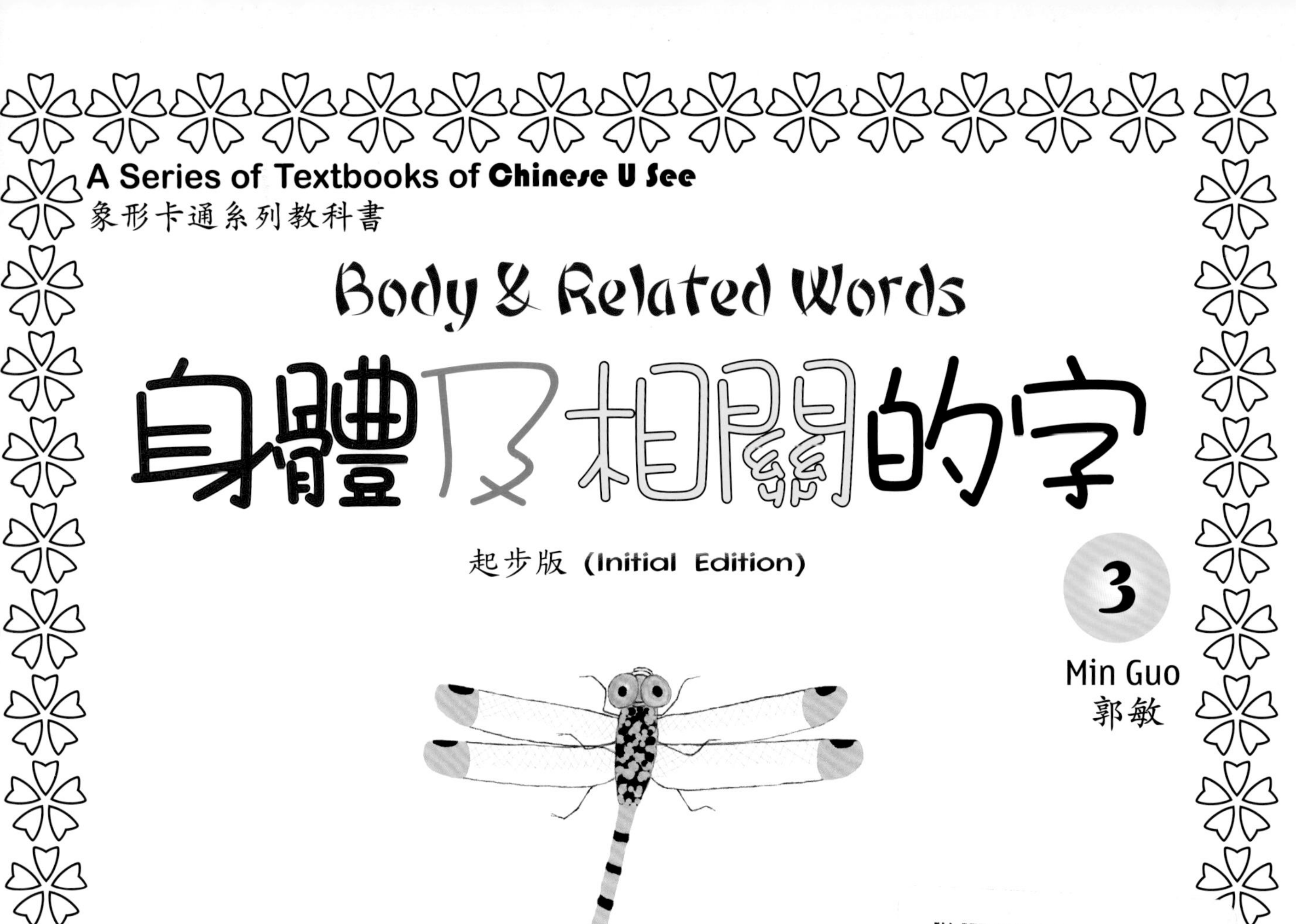

香港字藝出版社
Hong Kong Word Art Press

Body & Related Words 3 (*Initial Edition*) A Series of Textbooks of Chinese U Se

Author: Min Guo
Illustrator: Min Guo
Editors: Jin-li Li, Franklin Koo
Publisher: Hong Kong Word Art Press
Address: Unit 503, 5/F, Tower 2, Lippo Center, 89 Queensway Road, Admiralty, HK
Website: www.wordart.com.hk/www.chineseusee.com
Edition: First edition published in 2016, Hong Kong
Size: 210 mm × 190 mm
ISBN: 978-988-14915-5-8

身體及相關的字 3（起步版） 象形卡通系列教科書

作　　者：郭　敏
繪　　畫：郭　敏
編　　輯：李金麗，顧為傑
出　　版：香港字藝出版社
地　　址：香港金鐘金鐘道 89 號力寶中心第 2 座 5 樓 503 室
網　　頁：www.wordart.com.hk/www.chineseusee.com
版　　次：2016 年香港第一版第一次印刷
規　　格：210 mm × 190 mm
國際書號：978-988-14915-5-8

漢字難學的真正原因

是漢語有兩個系統：

1. 發音系統，由拼音作為學習工具。
2. 文字系統，沒有學習工具。一般的圖畫與漢字的筆畫和結構沒有任何關係，所以對漢字的書寫及記憶沒有任何幫助。

其他的主要原因是學科界限不清：

1. 字源學是研究古漢字的，屬於文字考古學，與現代漢字的學習沒有太大的關係。用甲骨文教現代漢字會使漢字更加難學。
2. 漢字是象形文字，而英文是拼音文字，英文的教學理念和教學法不能完全兼顧漢語學習（郭敏，2013）。

象形卡通

是根據現代漢字的象形特點、筆畫、字義、字形、結構和字與字的關係、參考歷史上某些相關的文獻、甲骨文殘餘的象形文字以及漢字的文化內涵所創作的。象形卡通給漢字學習提供了一個生動活潑的視覺教具，是漢語教學法上歷史性的突破。

郭敏，《漢字圖畫式教學》，2013 年香港大學首屆國際漢語教學大會會議論文。

Why is Chinese Very Difficult to Learn?

There are two systems for Chinese words:

1. The Phonetic System: Pinyin is the learning tool.
2. The Word System: There is no learning tool. Common pictures are not related to the strokes and structures of Chinese words, so they have nothing to do with word writing and recognition.

The other major reasons are that the diciplines are blended:

1. Etymology is a study of ancient pictographs, which are totally different from modern Chinese words. Using ancient words to teach modern Chinese will make it even more difficult and confusing to learn Chinese.
2. Chinese is a pictographic language, and English is a phonetic language. English teaching theories and approaches cannot totally compatible with learning the Chinese language (Min Guo, 2013).[1]

Pictographic Cartoons

are created according to the pictographic characteristics of modern Chinese words, their strokes, meanings, structures, related historical documents, cultural content and the connections among the words. Pictographic Cartoons provide vivid and profound learning tools. It is a historical breakthrough in Chinese teaching and learning methodology.

1.Min Guo, "The Methodology of Learning Chinese with Word Cartoons", 2013. The First International Conference for Chinese Teaching in Hong Kong University.

Table of Contents
目錄

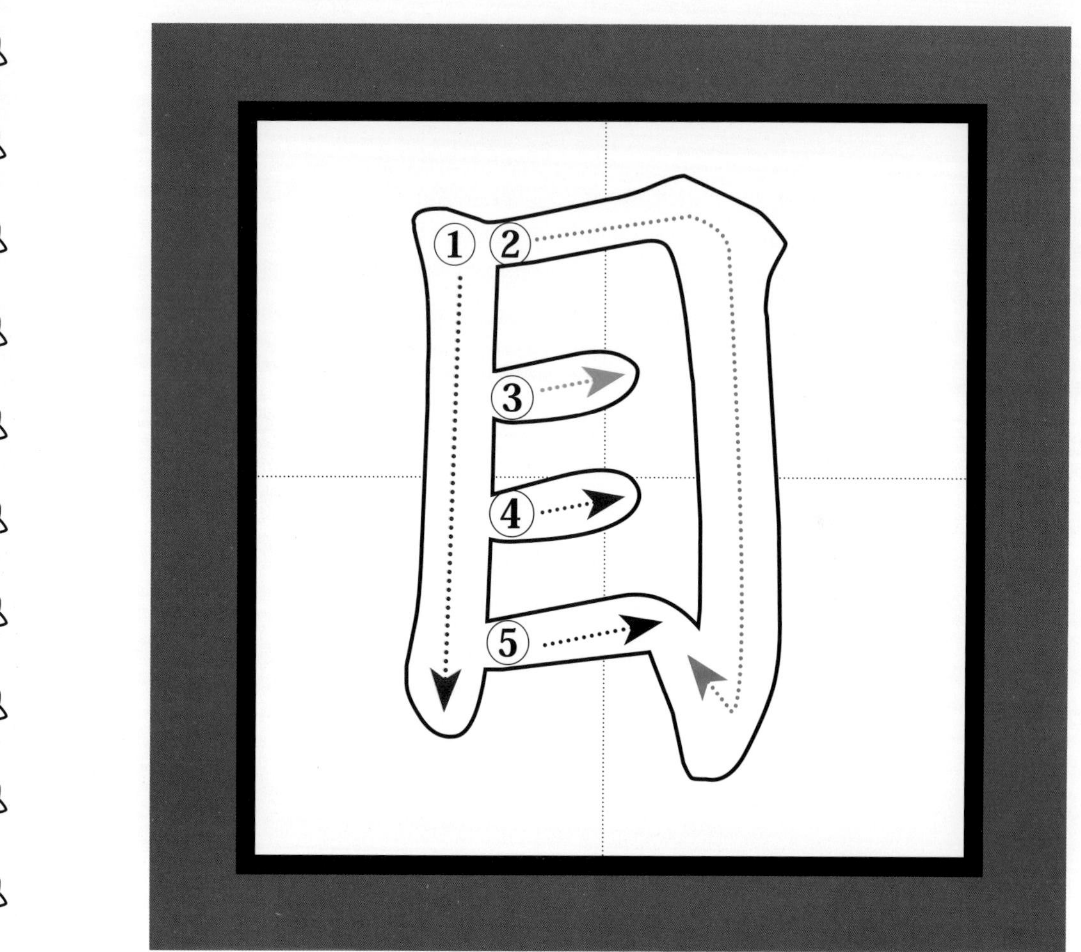

1
2
3
4
5

Lesson One 第一課

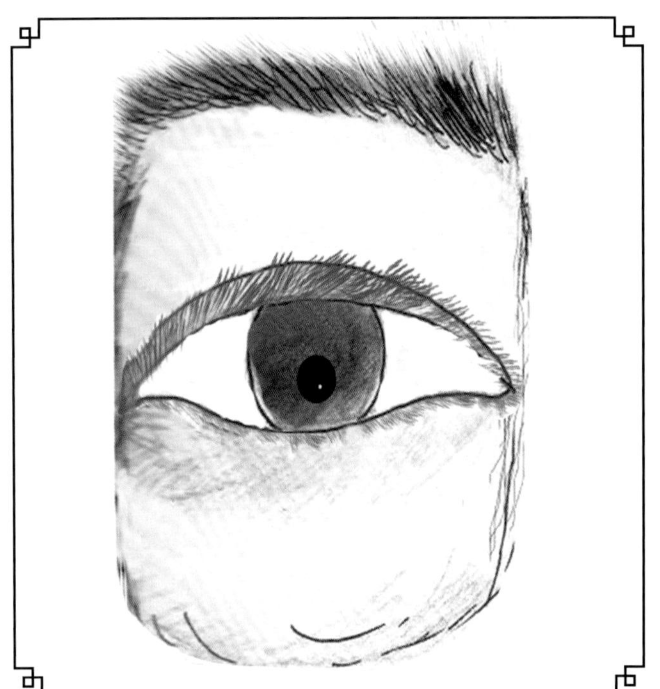

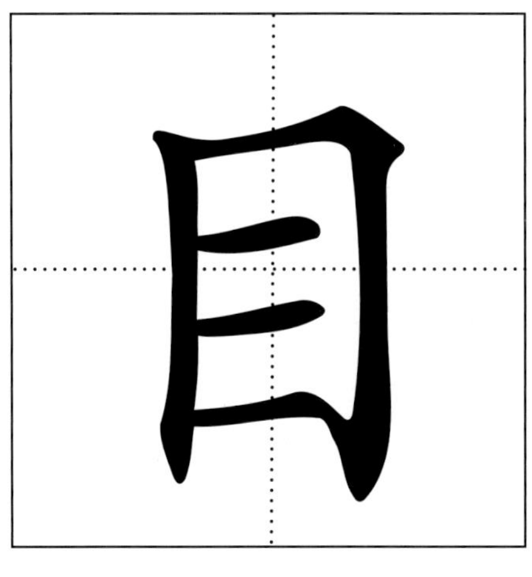

eye

mù	guāng
目	光

sight/gaze

光
1
2
3
4
5
6

guāng

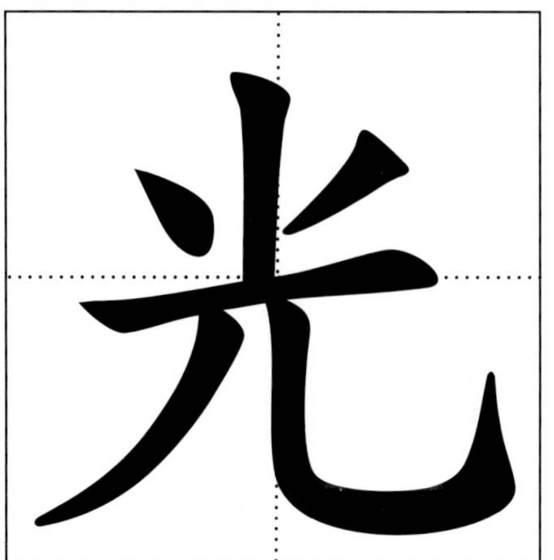

light

dēng	guāng
燈	光

lamplight

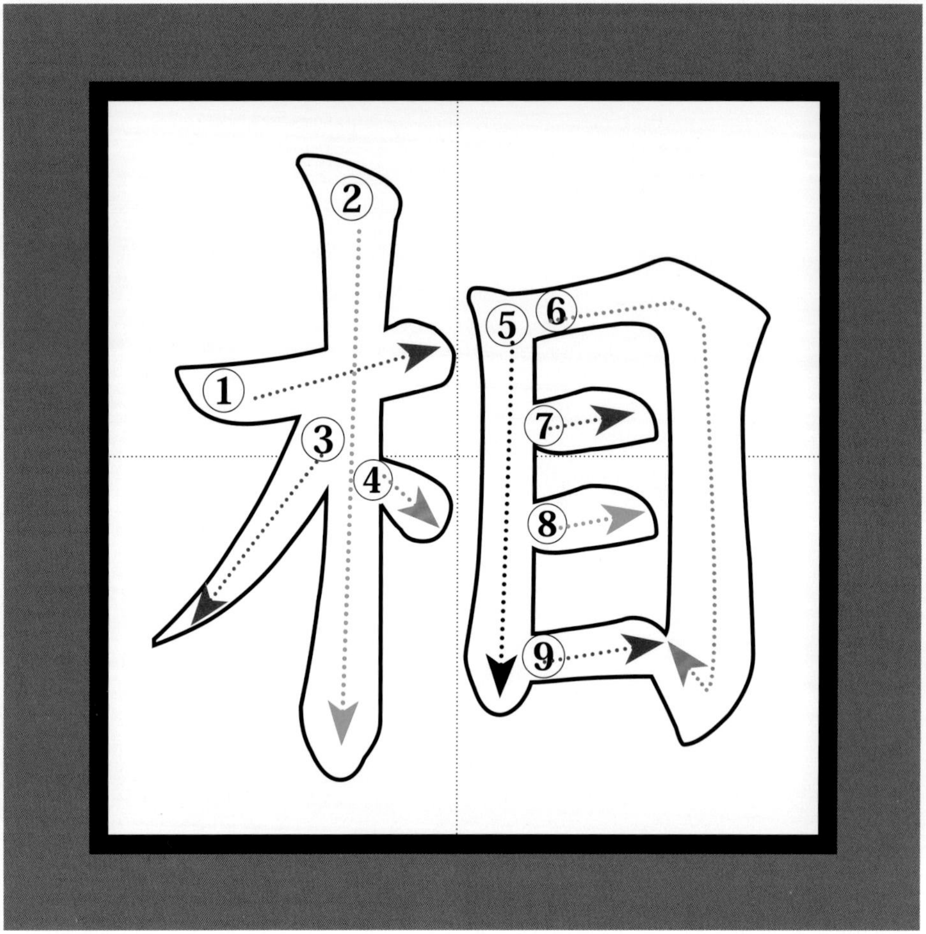

相

1 2 3 4 5 6 7 8 9

xiàng

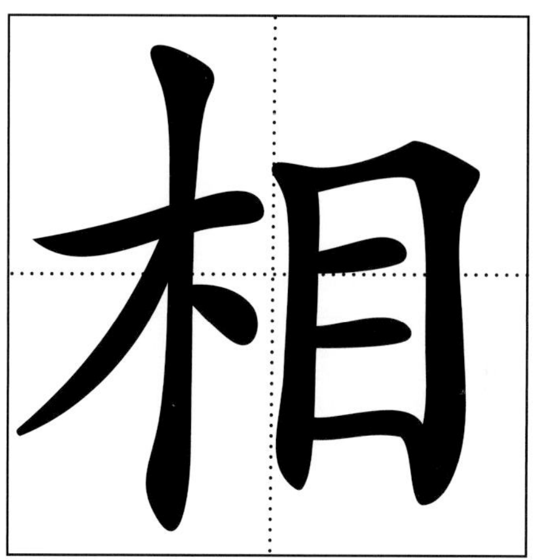

observe/look

xiàng	mào
相	貌

appearance

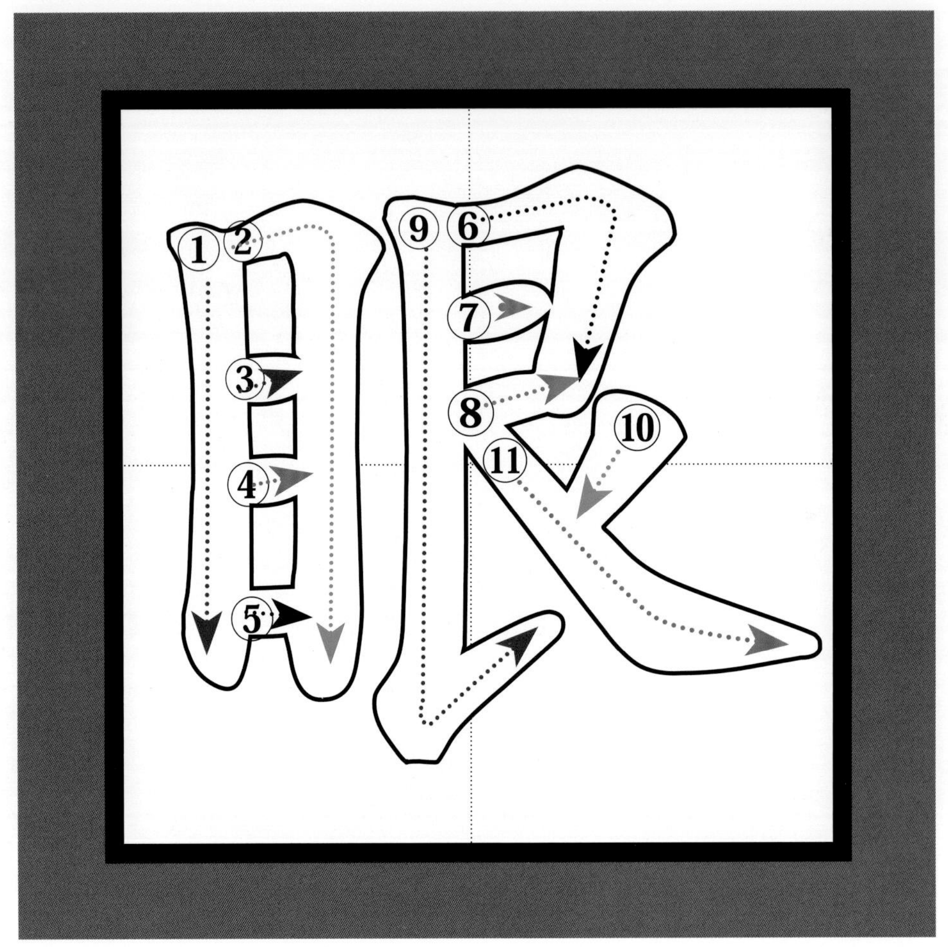

1
2
3
4
5
6
7
8
9
10
11

yǎn

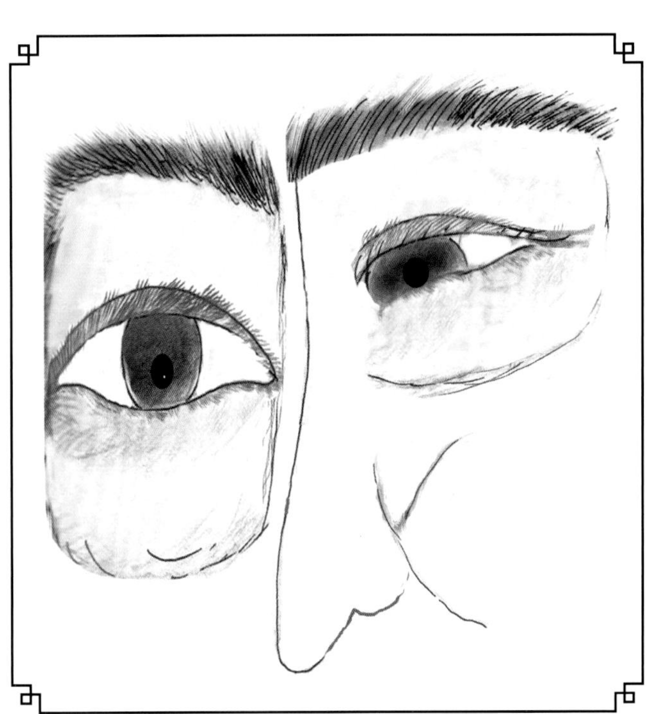

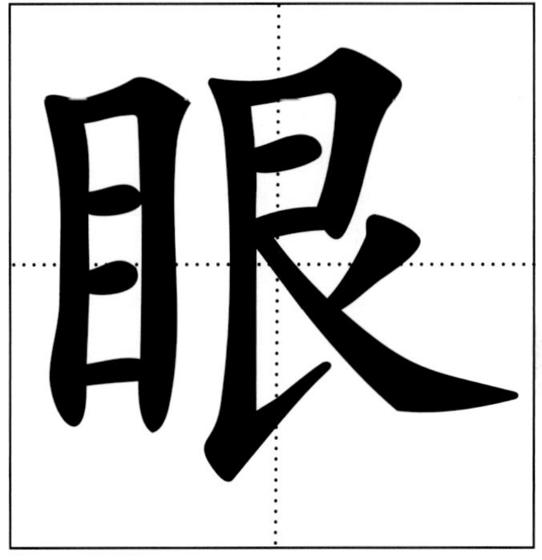

eye

yǎn	jing
眼	睛

eye

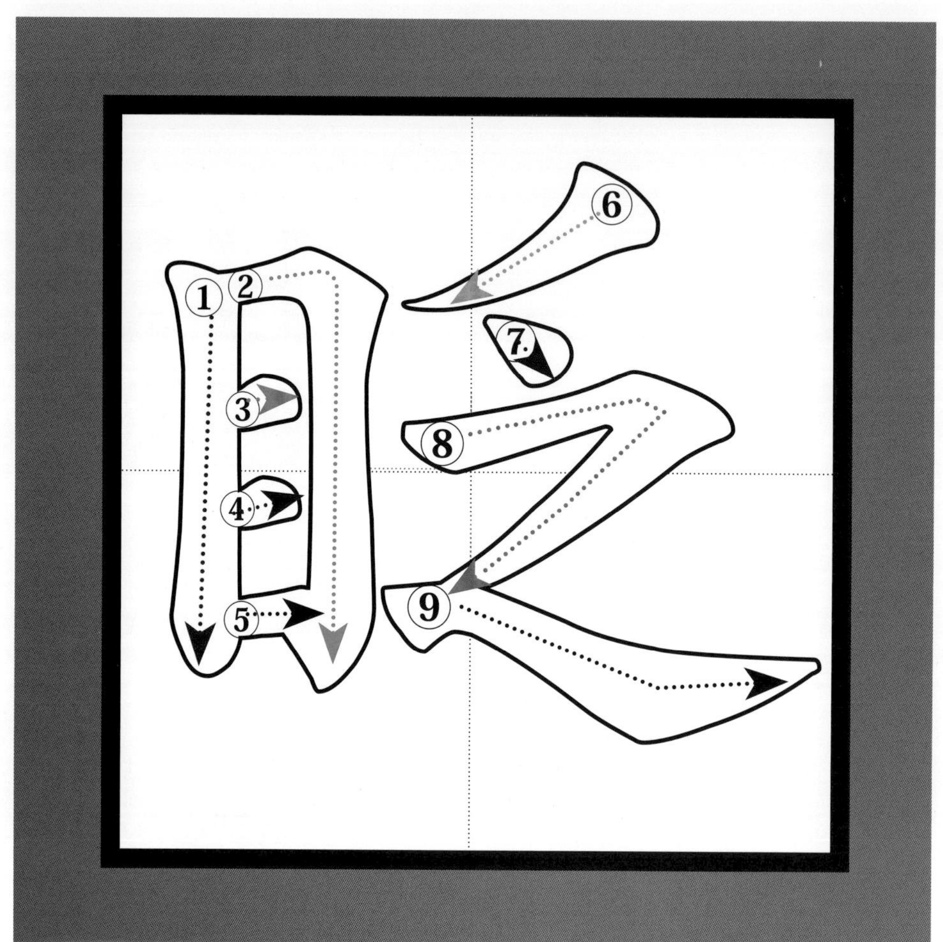
1
2
3
4
5
6
7
8
9

zhǎ

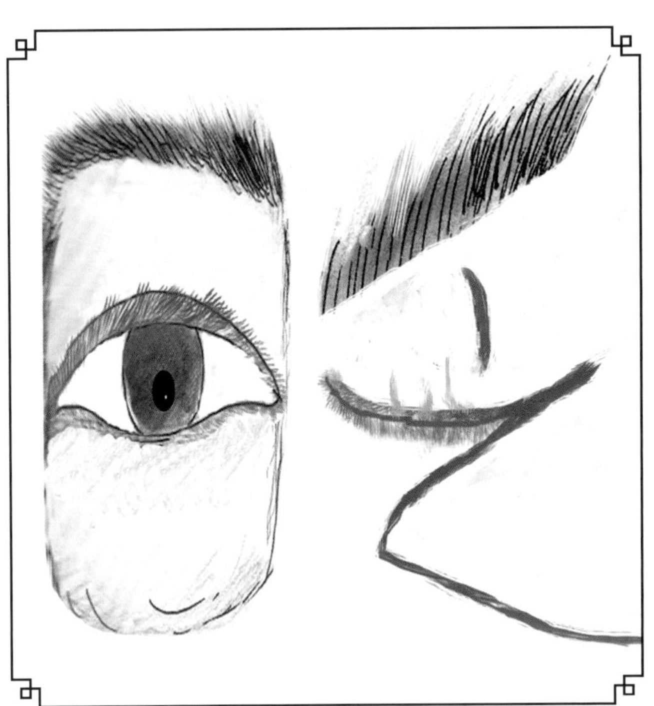

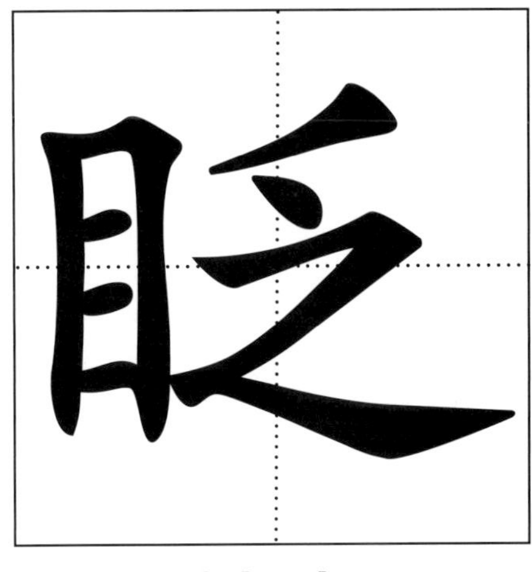

blink

zhǎ	yǎn
眨	眼

wink

Read these words.
讀一讀這些字。

dīng

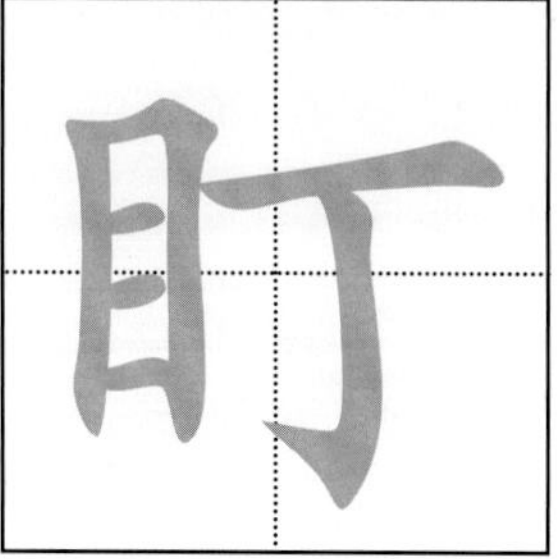

fix one's eyes on

pàn

long for

shuì

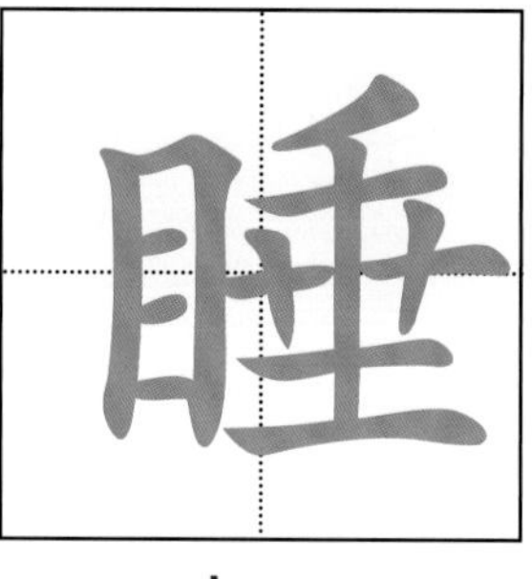

sleep

miáo

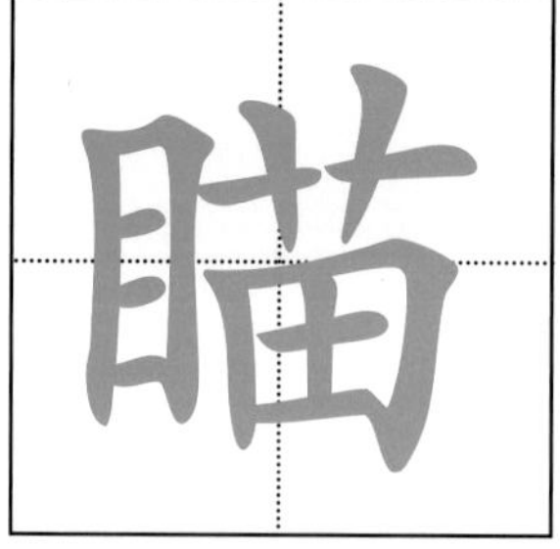

set sight on

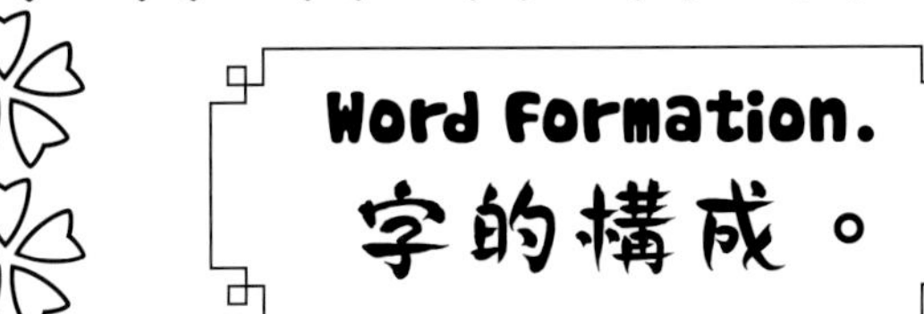

Word Formation.
字的構成。

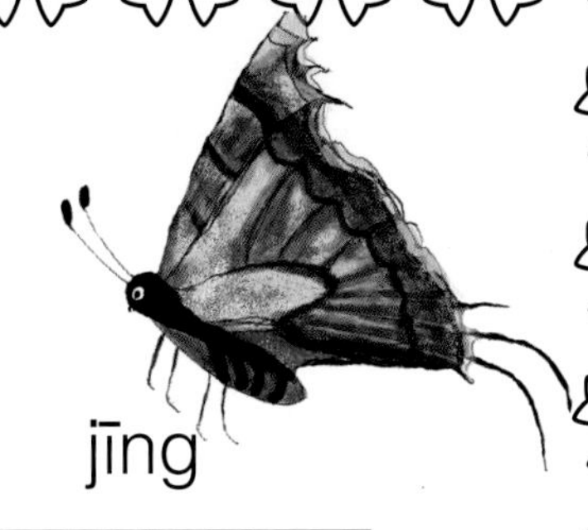

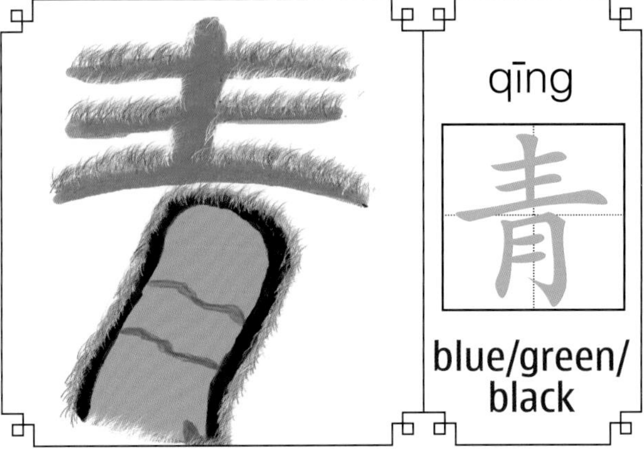

jīng

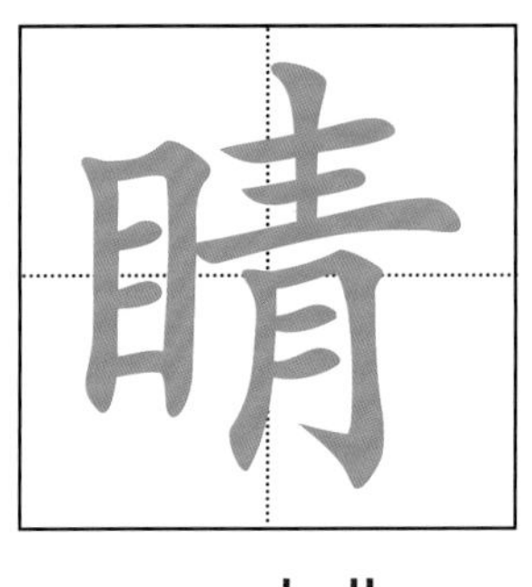

eyeball

look/glance at

1
2
3
4
5
6
7
8
9

kàn

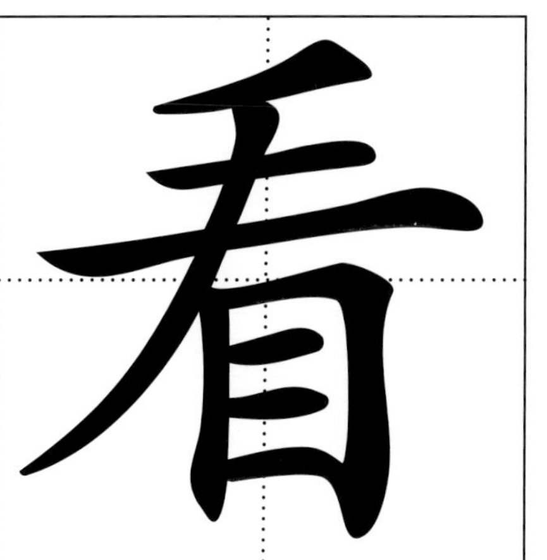

look/watch/see

kàn	zhe
看	着

look at

1
2
3
4
5
6
7
8
9
10

chà

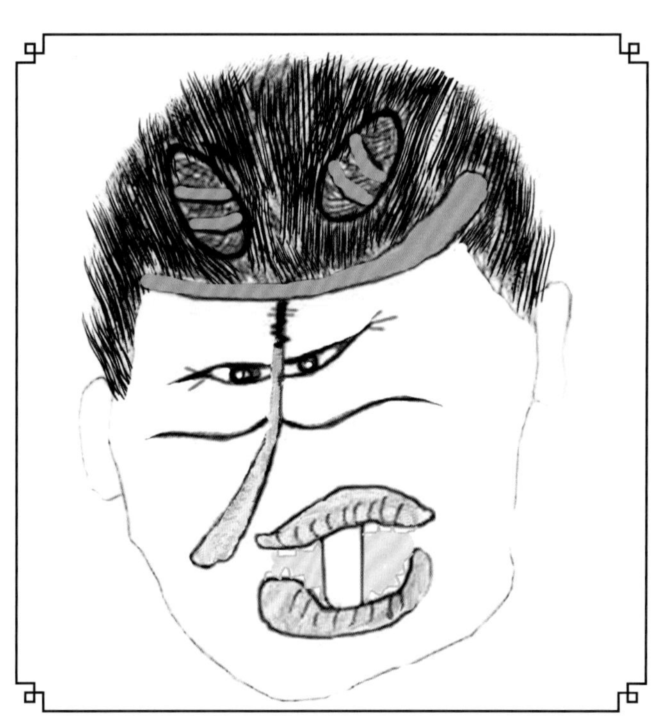

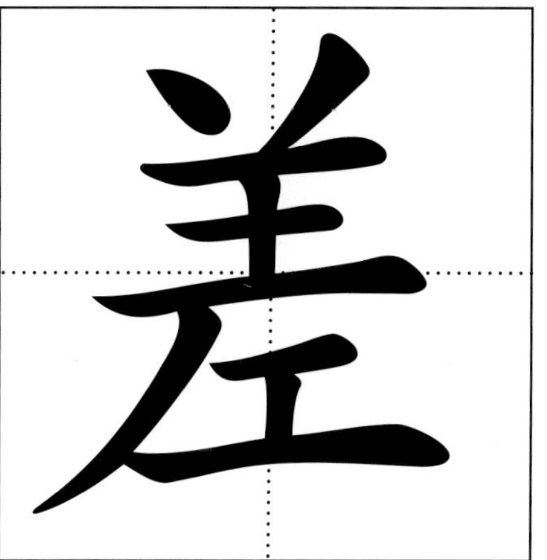

差

mistake/errand

chū	chāi
出	差

ona a business trip

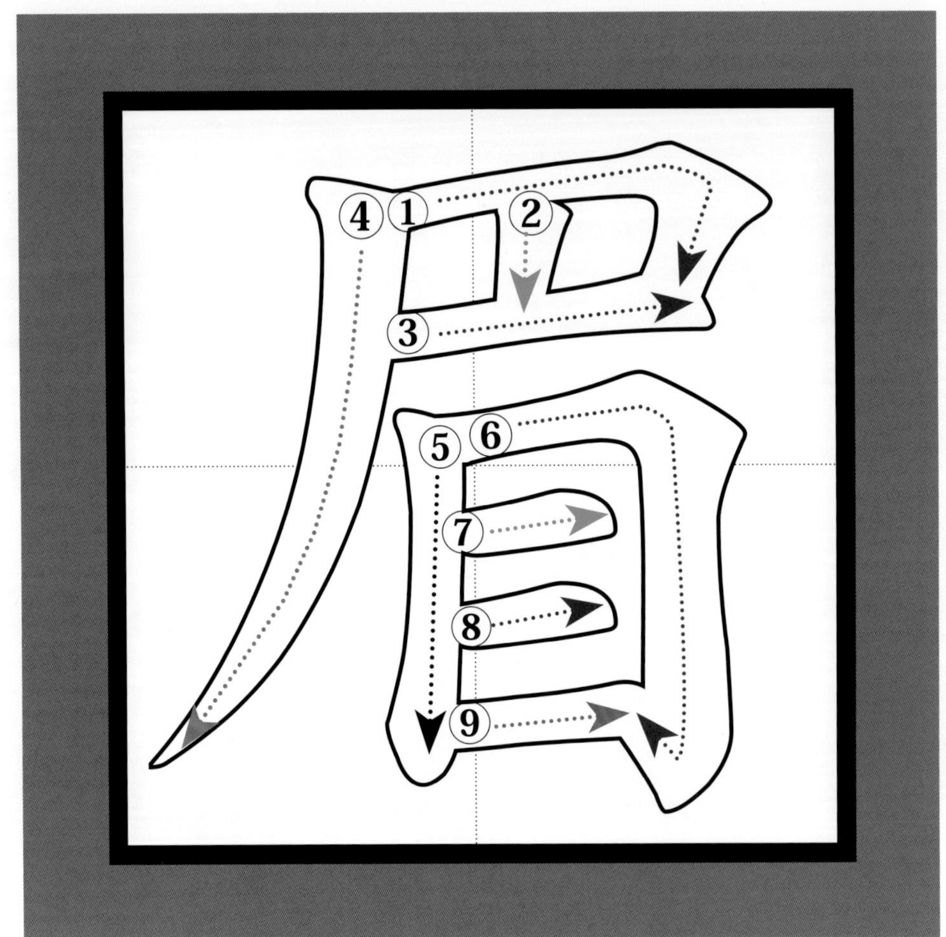

4
1
2
3
5
6
7
8
9

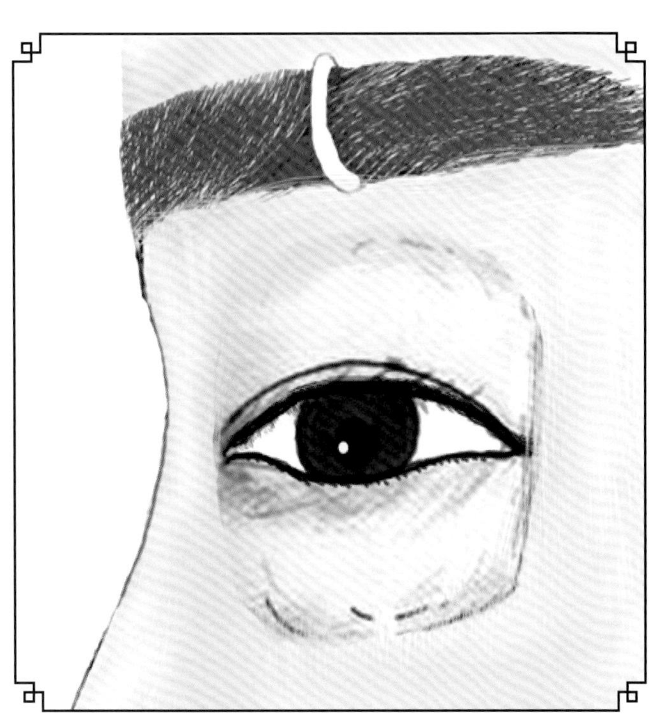

méi

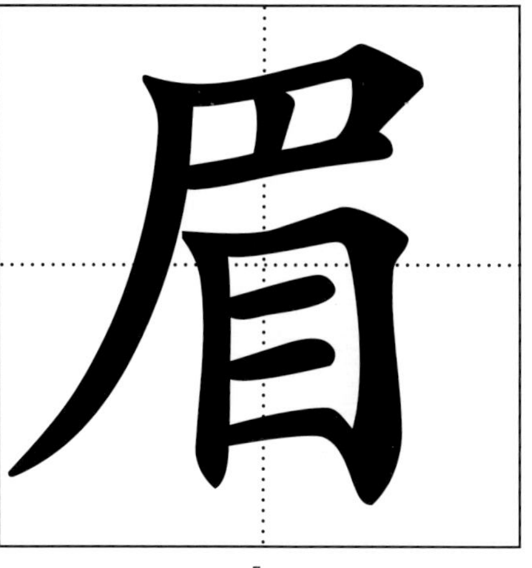

eyebrow

méi	mao
眉	毛

eyebrows

1
2
3
4

máo

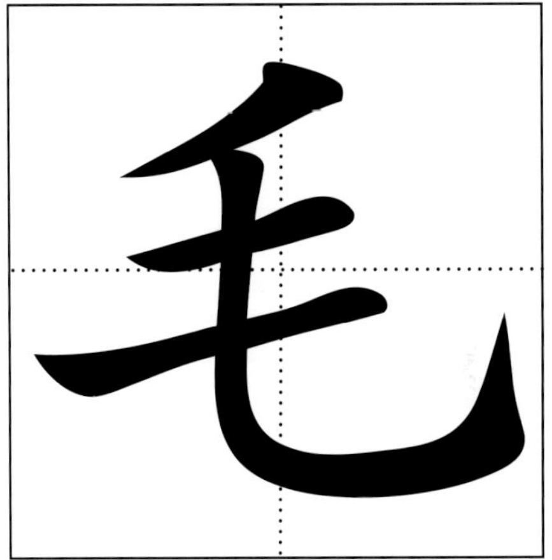

hair/wool

hàn	máo
汗	毛

fine hair on a human body

1
2
3
4
5
6
7
8
10
9
11
12
13
14

bí

nose

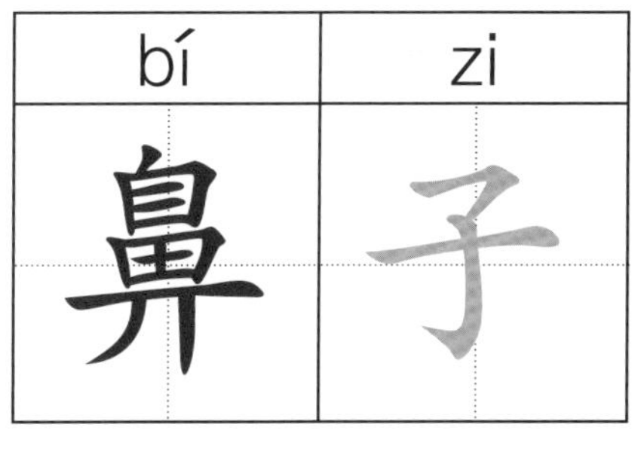

nose

Word Formation.

字的構成。

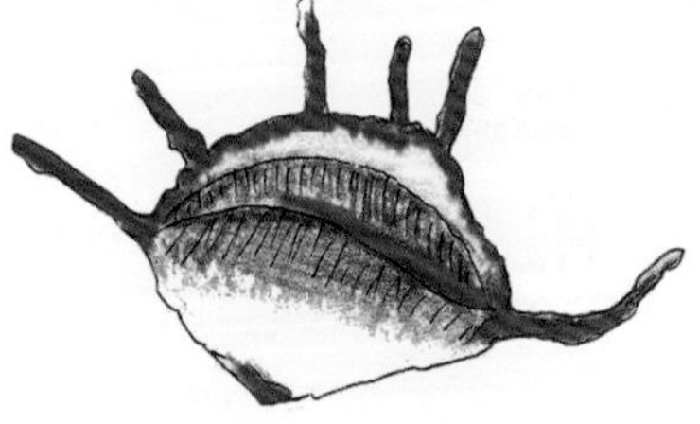

tóu

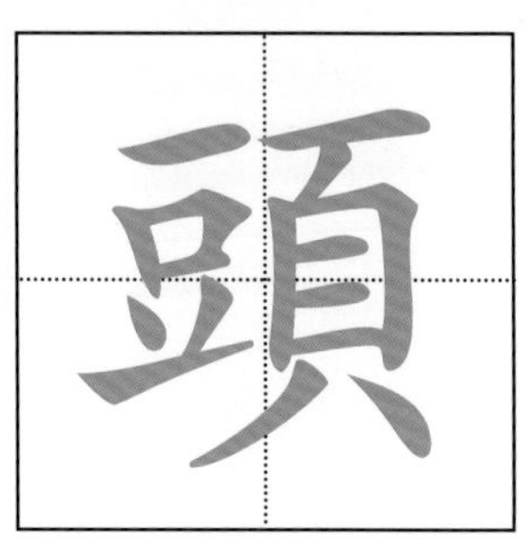

head

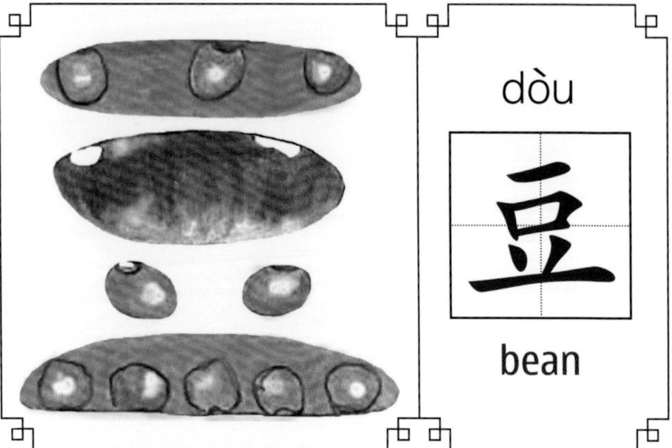

dòu

豆

bean

sī

think

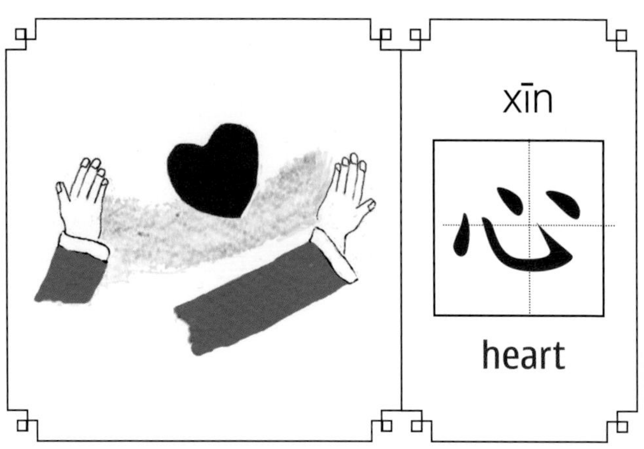

xīn

心

heart

What do we feel with?
用甚麼感覺事物？

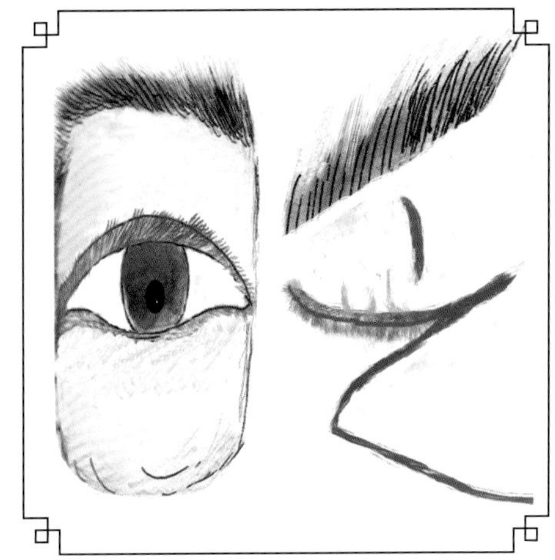

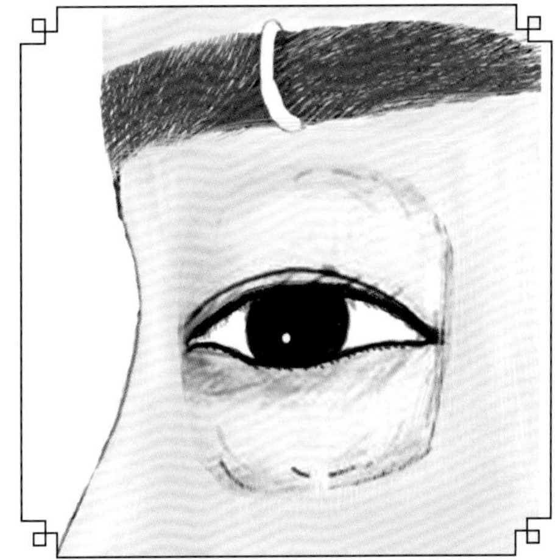

眉光眐鼻

1
2
3
4
5
6
7
8
9
10
11
12
13
14
15
16

Lesson Two 第二課

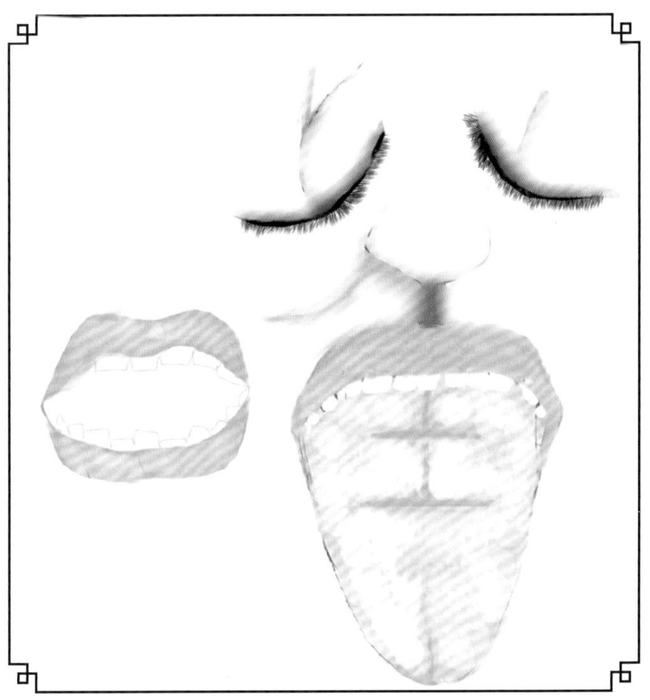

zuǐ

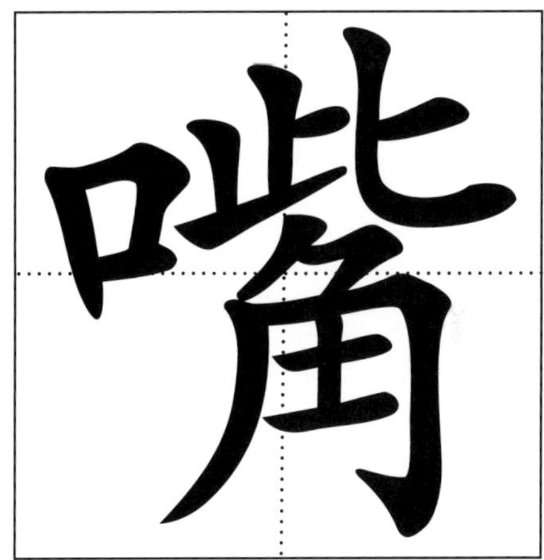

mouth

zuǐ	ba
嘴	巴

mouth

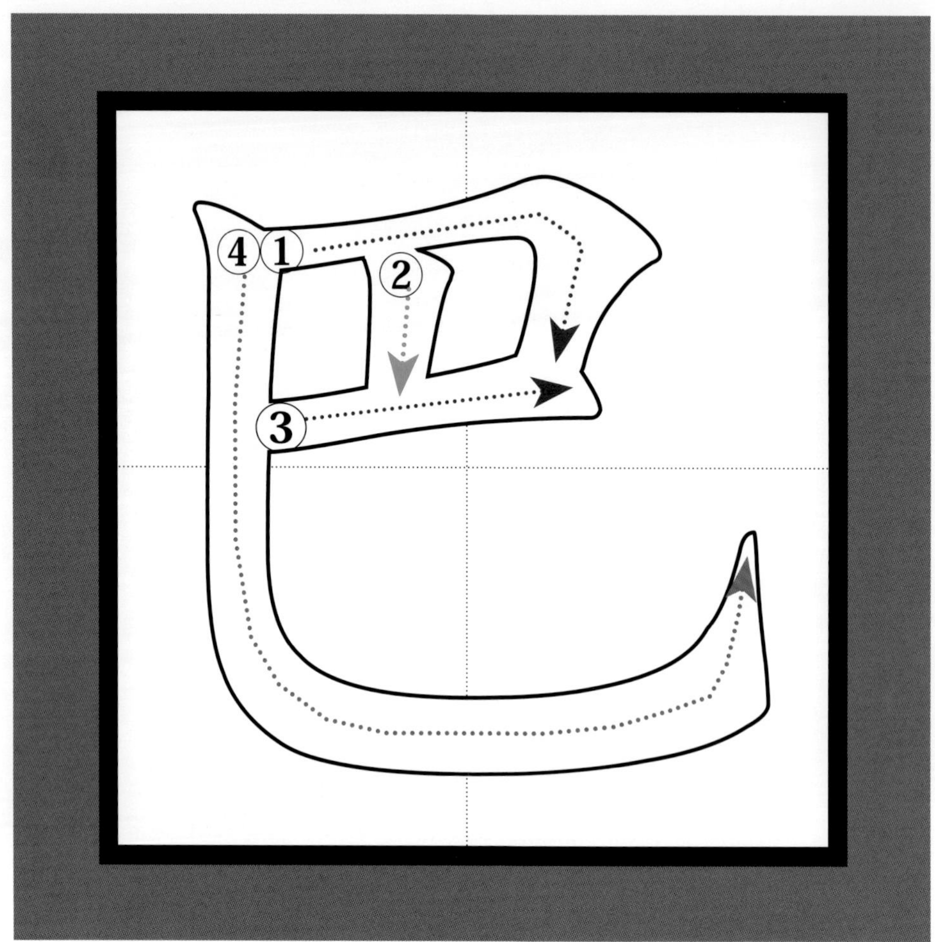
4
1
2
3

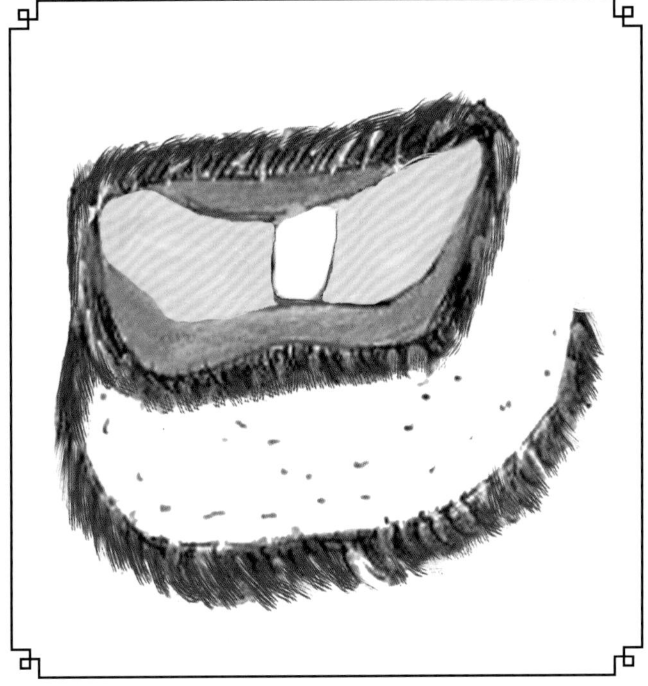

bā

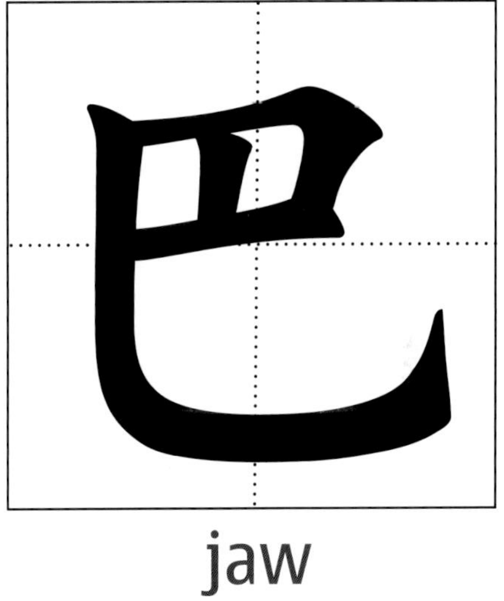

jaw

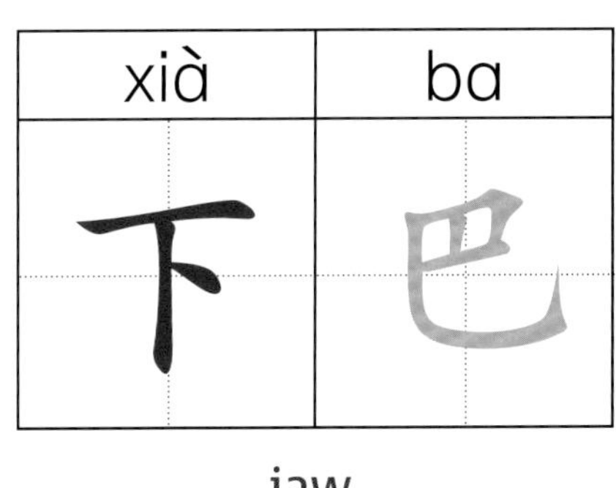

jaw

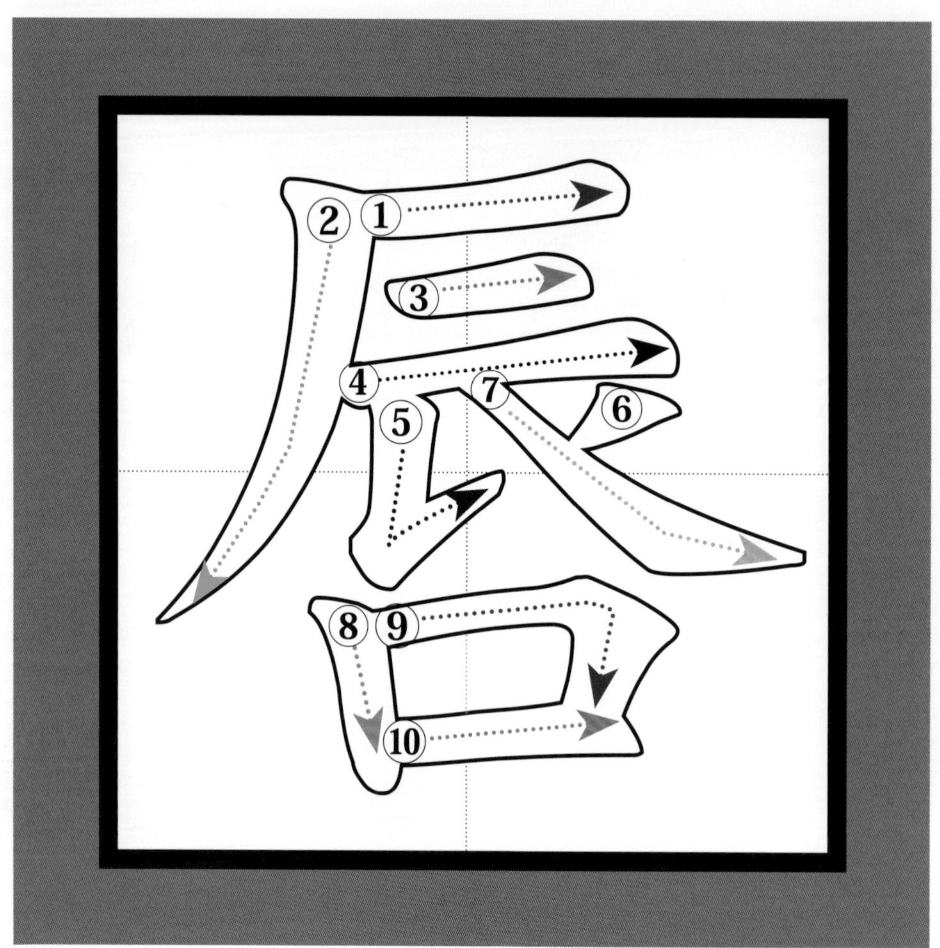
1
2
3
4
5
6
7
8
9
10

chún

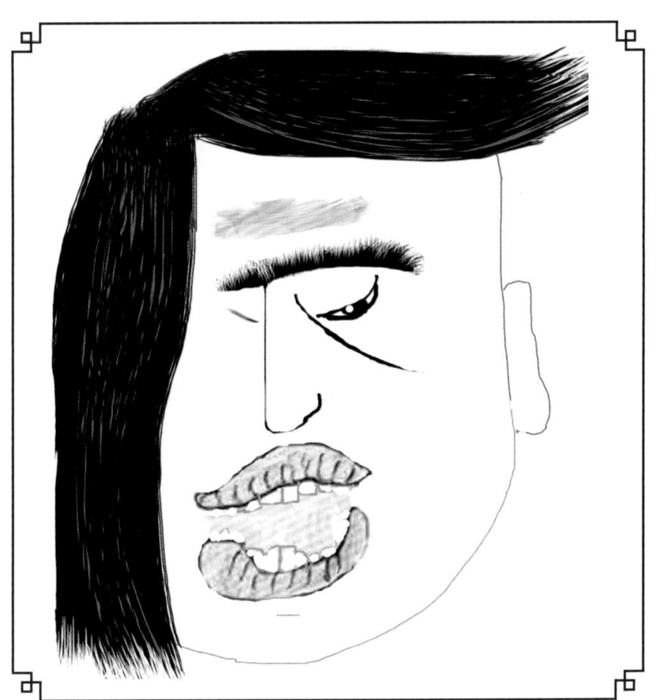

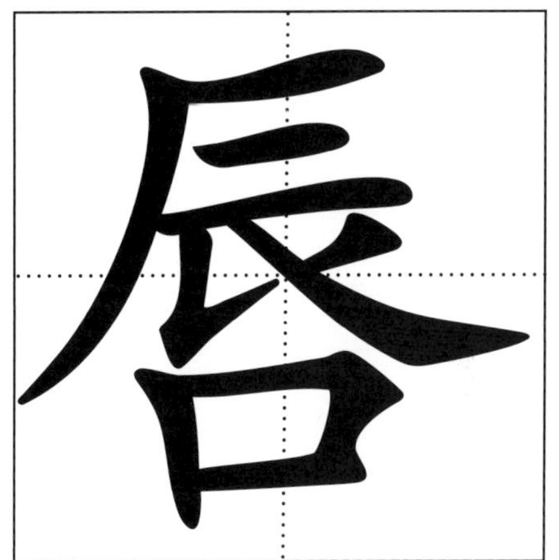

lip

zuǐ	chún
嘴	唇

lips

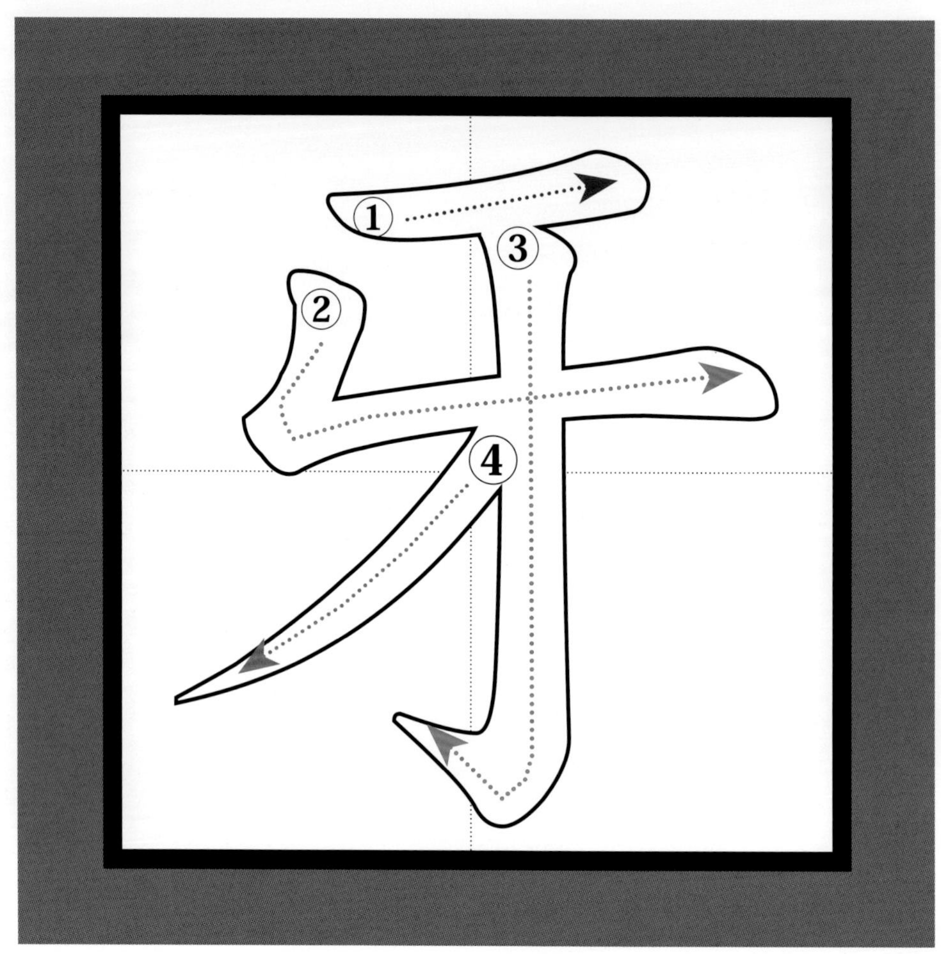

1
2
3
4

yá

牙

teeth/tooth

quǎn	yá
犬	牙

canine teeth

2. Ancient Chinese had a custom of replacing their teeth with animals'. 中國古代有拔牙和安上獸牙的風俗。

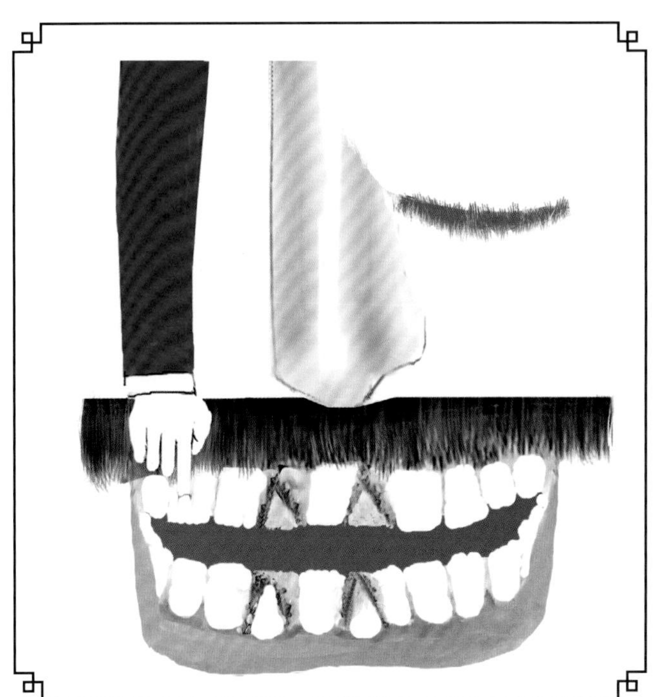

chǐ

tooth

yá	chǐ
牙	齒

teeth

Word Formation.
字的構成。

kōng

空

hollow/ empty

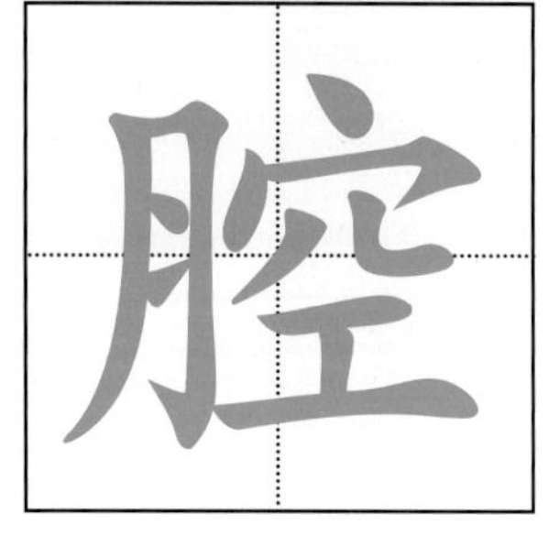

chest

lì

力

labour/ power

ribs

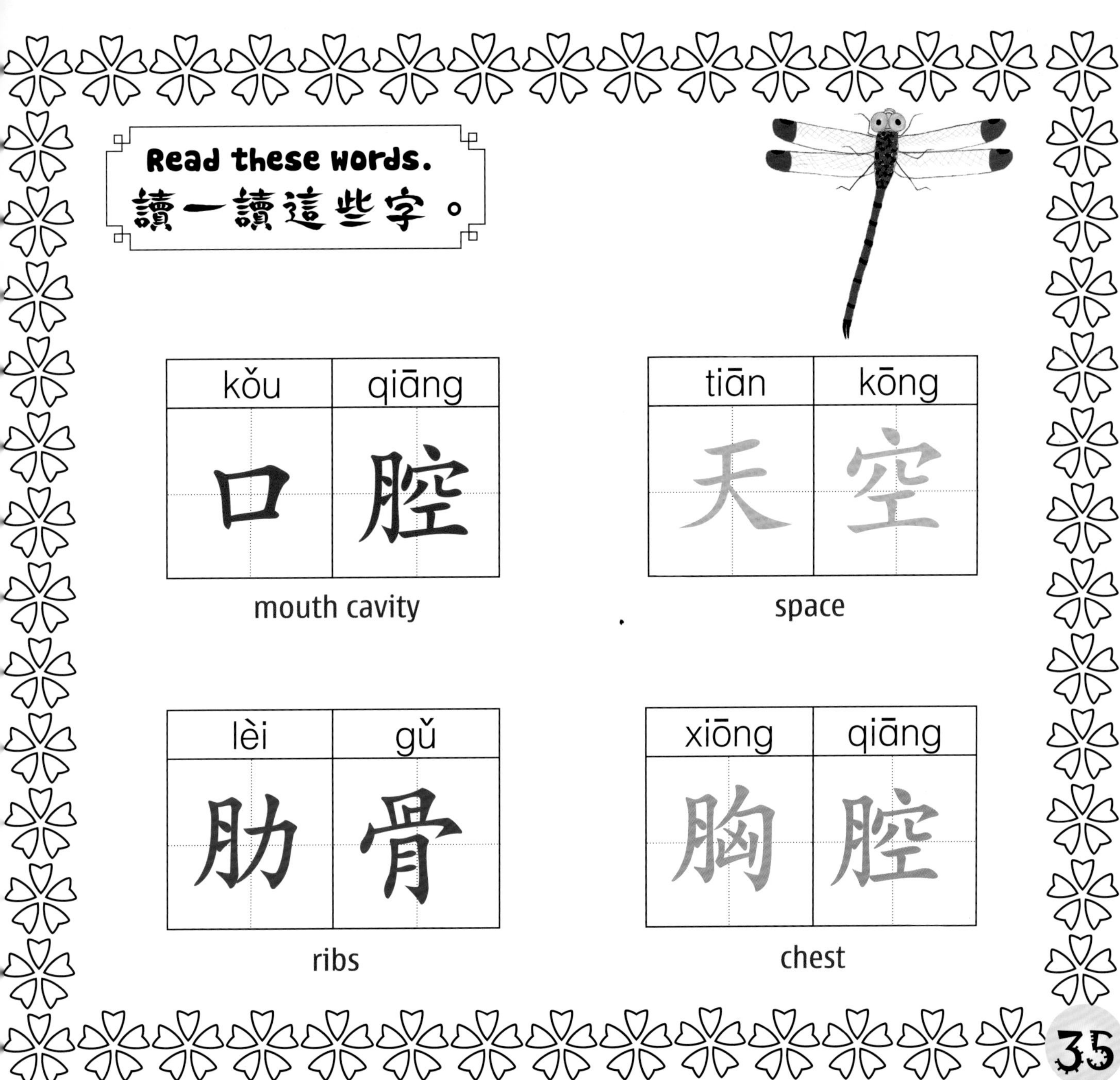

Read these words.
讀一讀這些字。

kǒu	qiāng
口	腔

mouth cavity

tiān	kōng
天	空

space

lèi	gǔ
肋	骨

ribs

xiōng	qiāng
胸	腔

chest

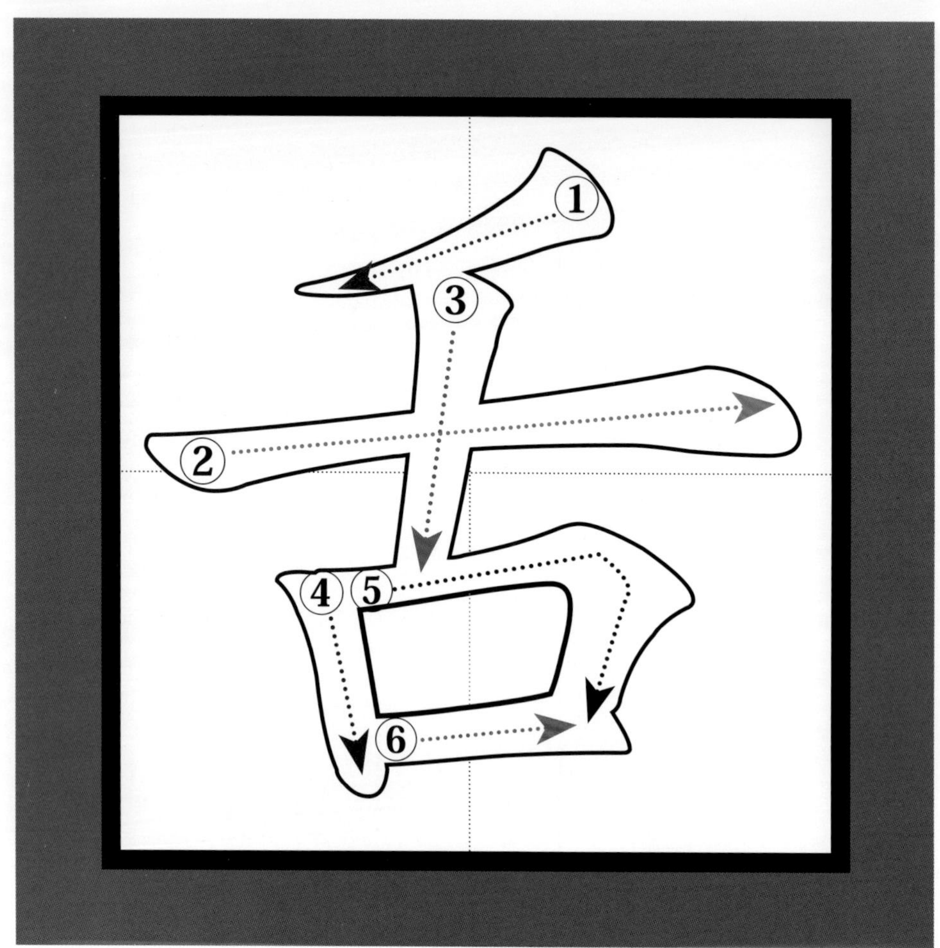
1
2
3
4
5
6

shé

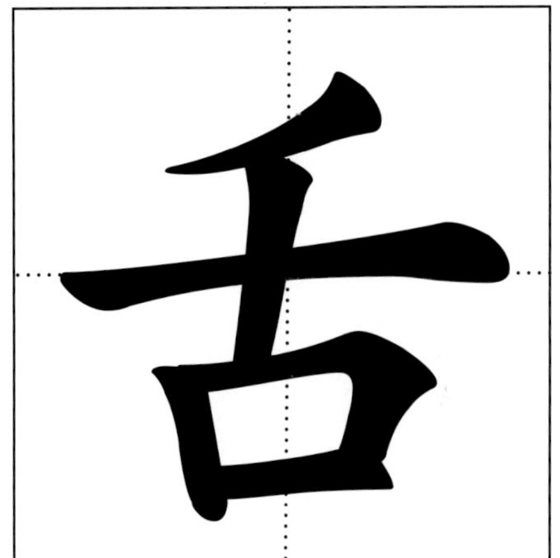

tongue

shé	tou
舌	頭

tongue

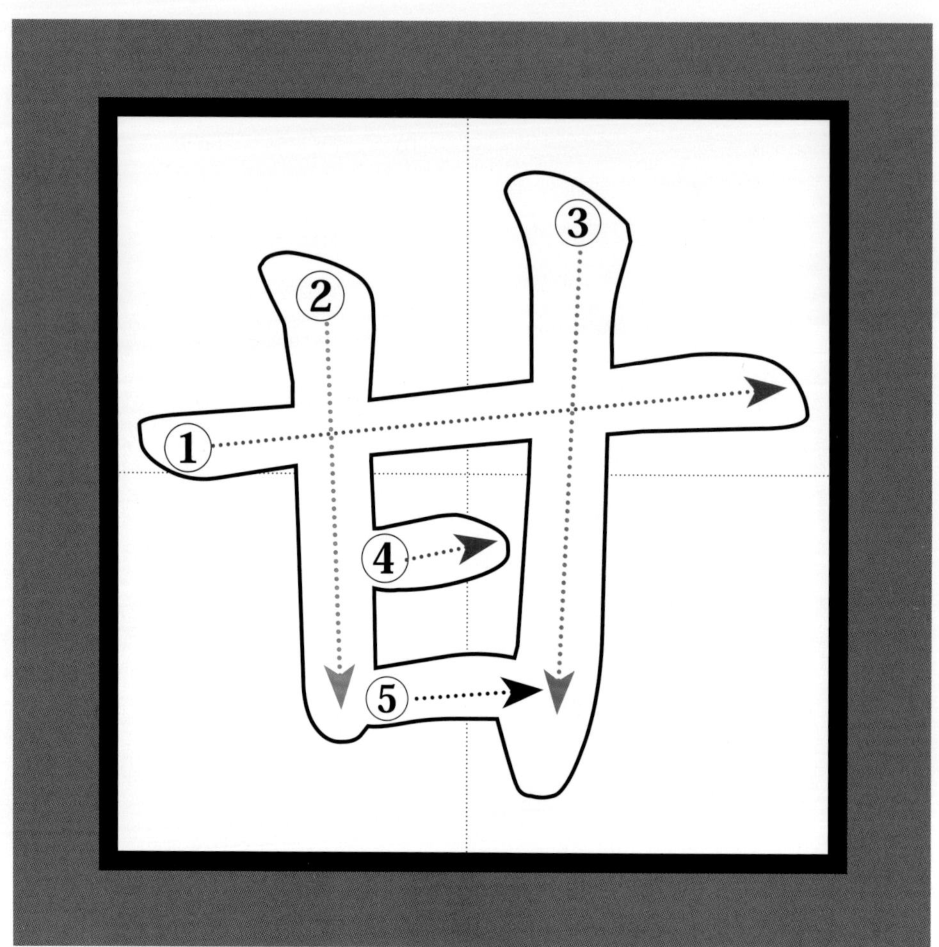
1
2
3
4
5

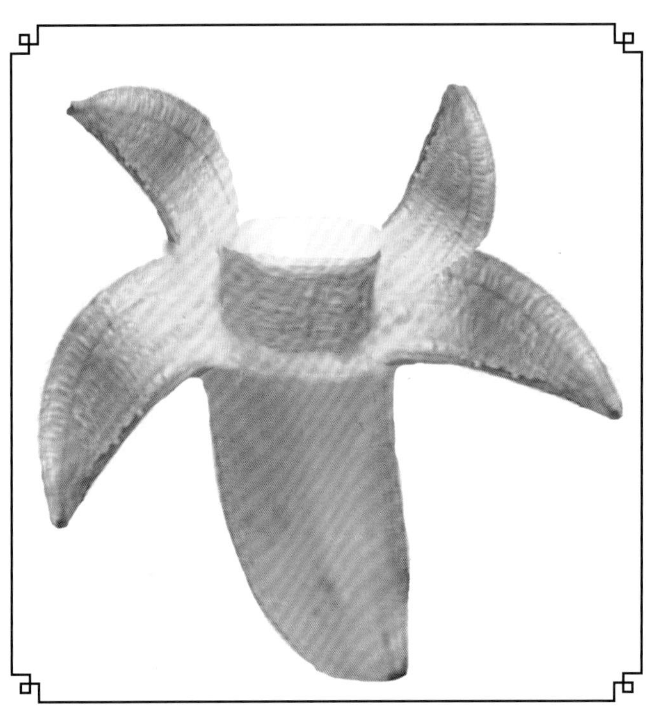

gān

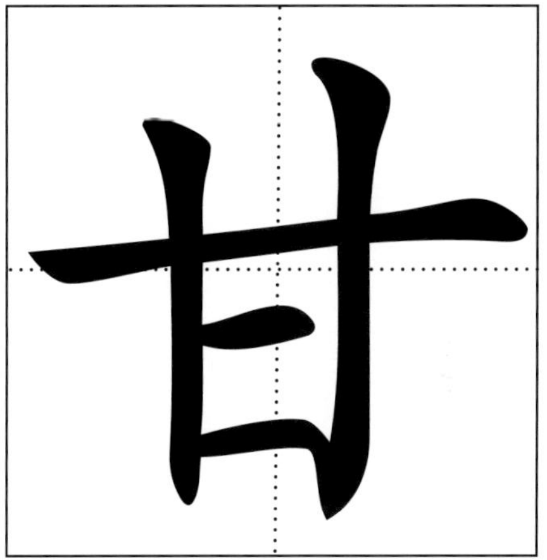

sweet/voluntary

gān	lù
甘	露[3]

honeydew/banana

3. Termniology for banana is " 甘露 ". 香蕉的學名是甘露。

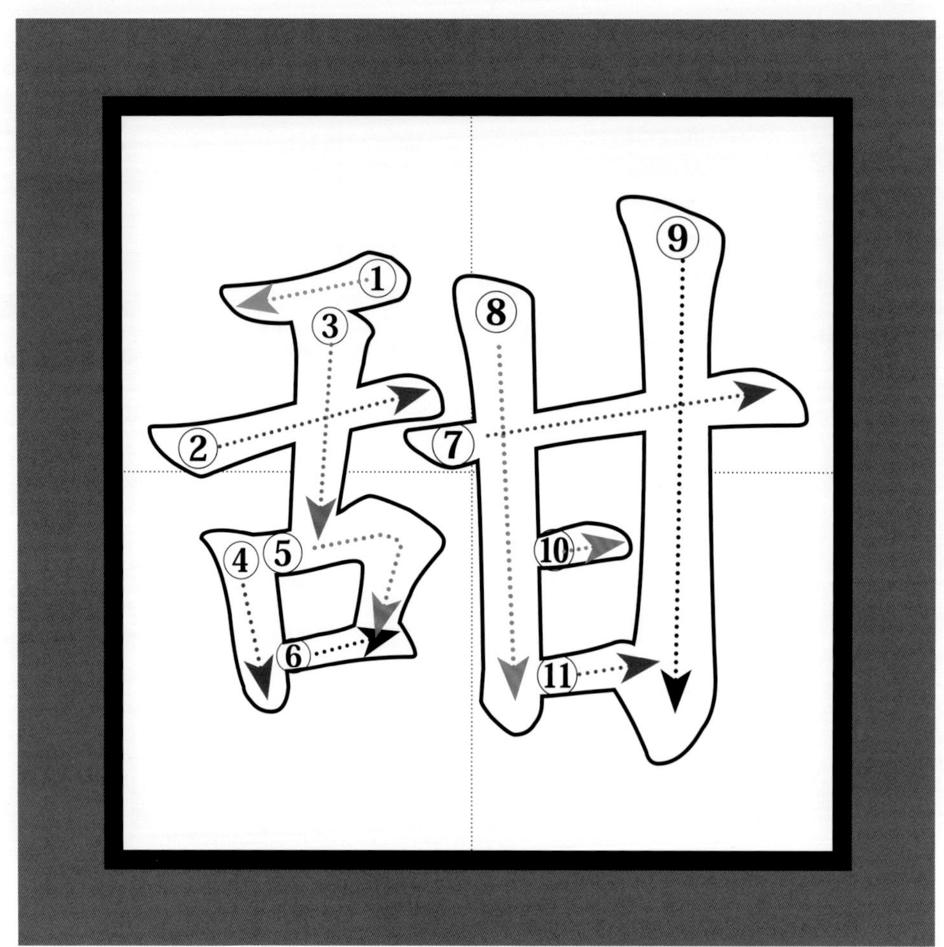
1
2
3
4
5
6
7
8
9
10
11

tián

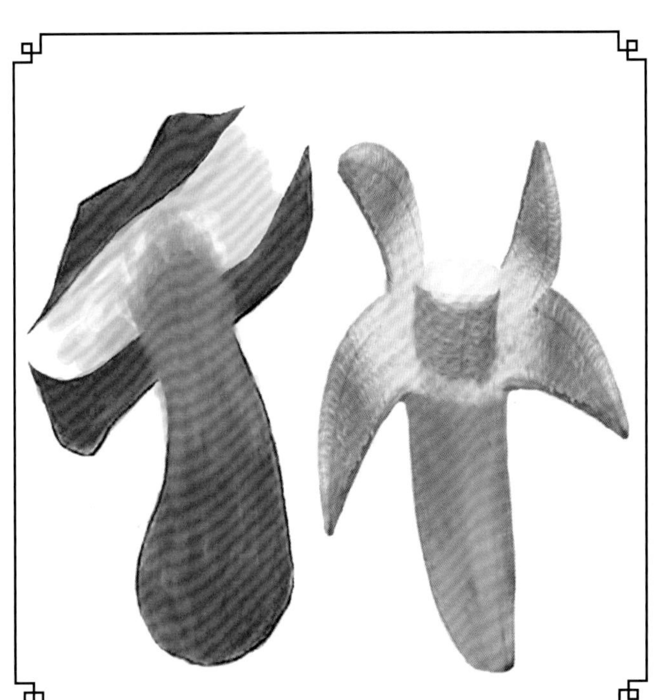

sweet

tián	mì
甜	蜜

sweet/happy

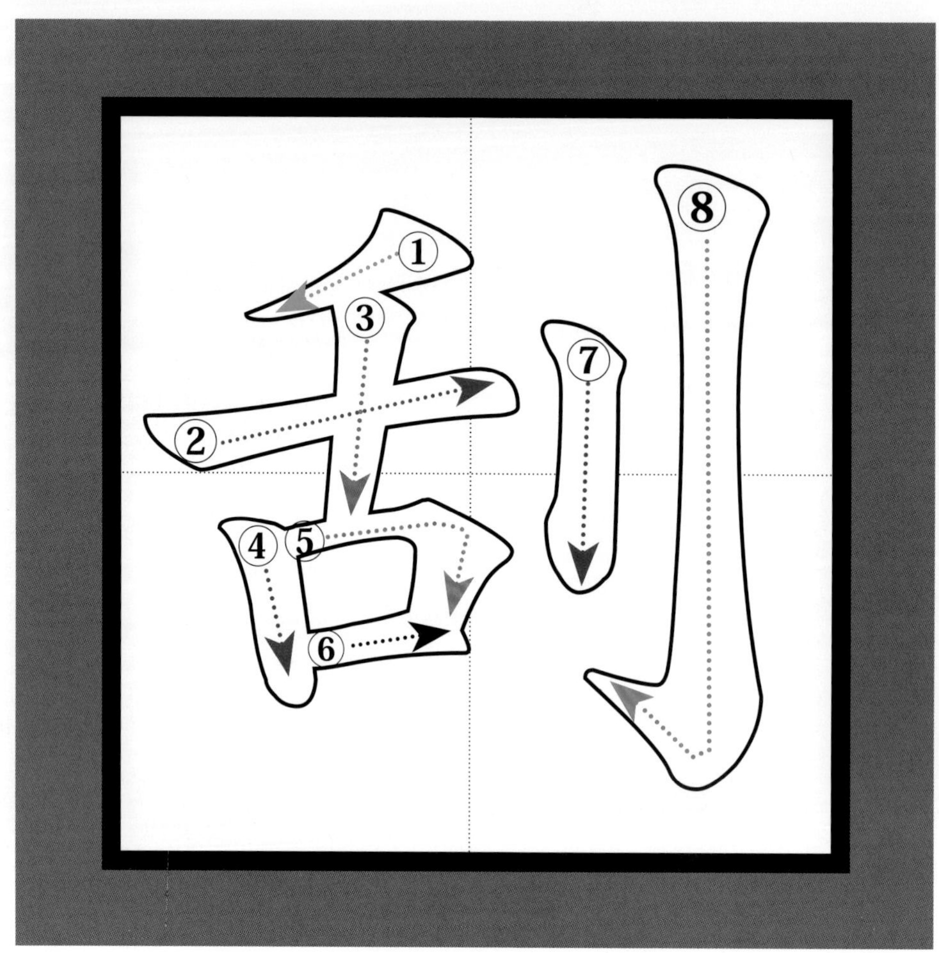
刮
1
2
3
4
5
6
7
8

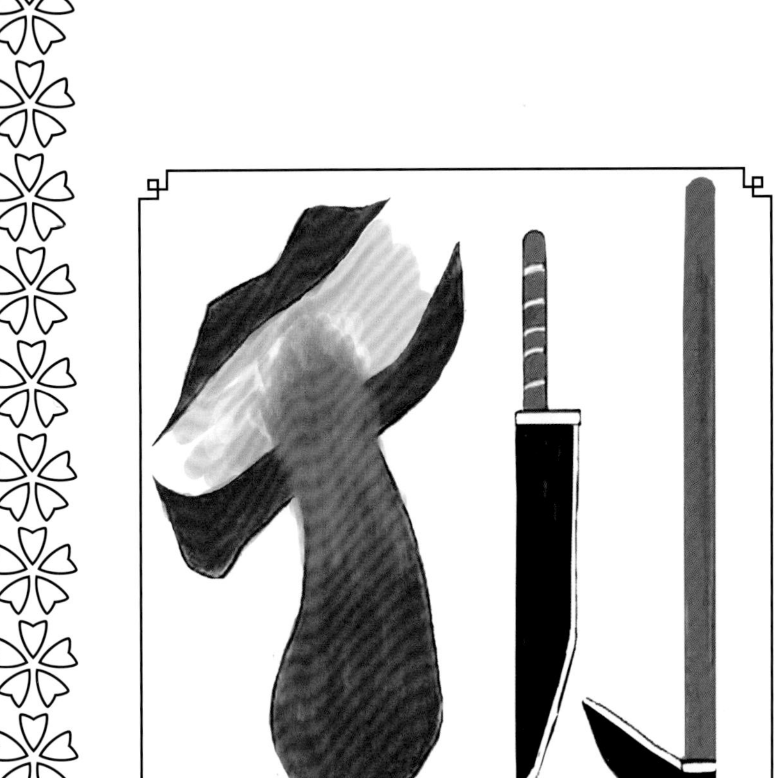

guā

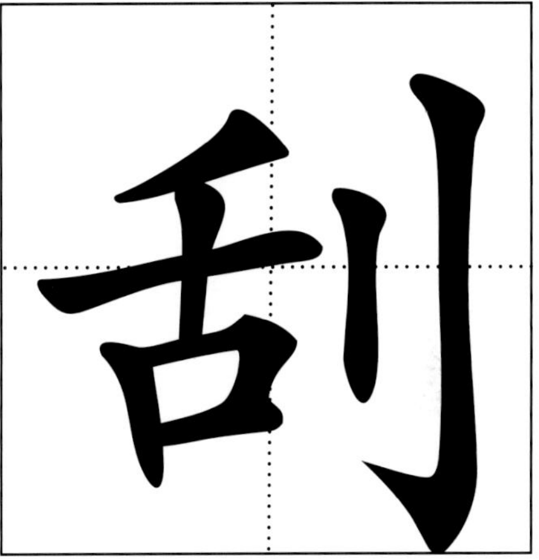

scrape

guā	diào
刮	掉

scrape out

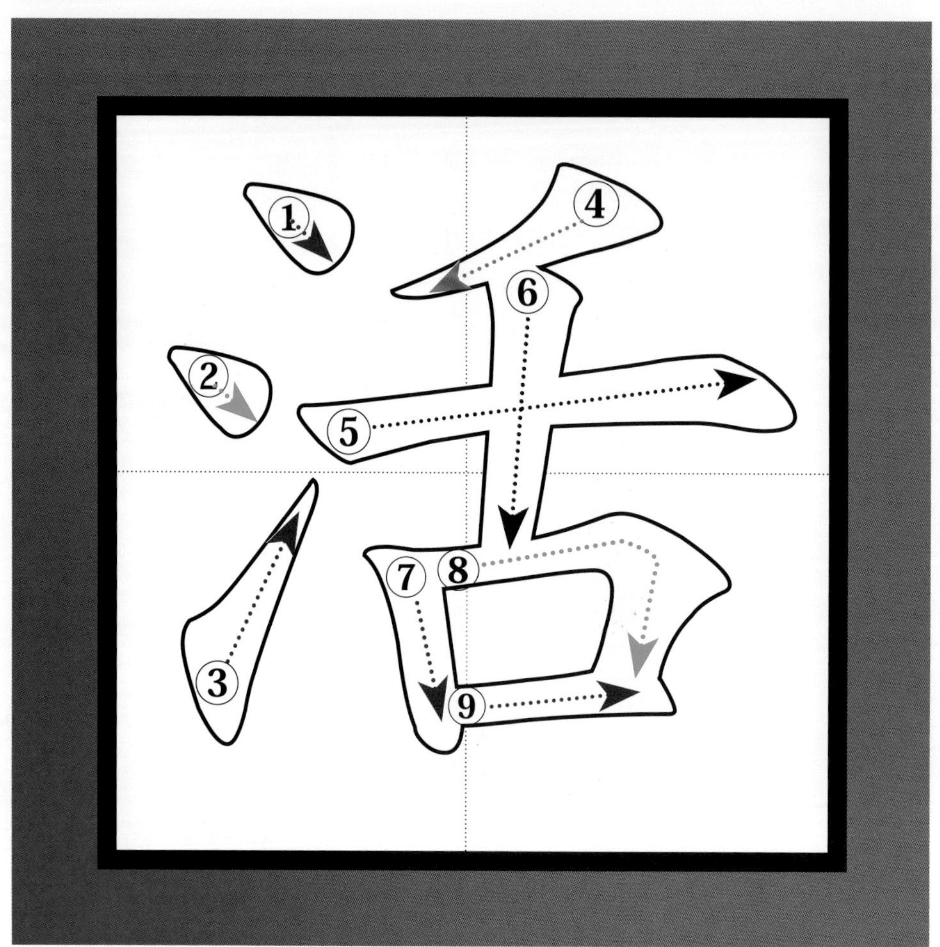
1
2
3
4
5
6
7
8
9

huó

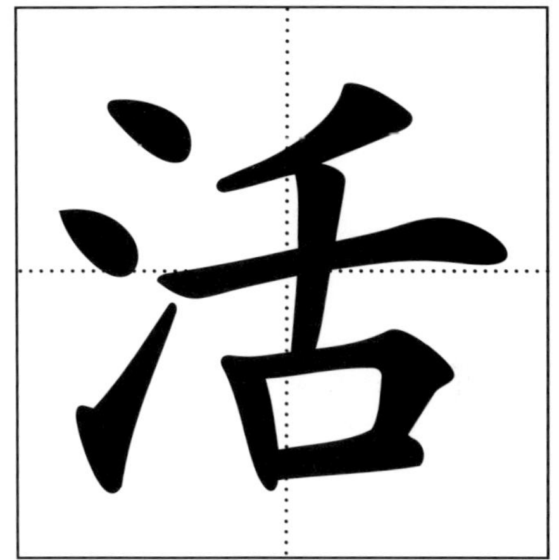

alive

shēng	huó
生	活

life

Read these words.
讀一讀這些字。

huà

話

talks/words

tián

恬

tranquil

tiǎn

lick

yá

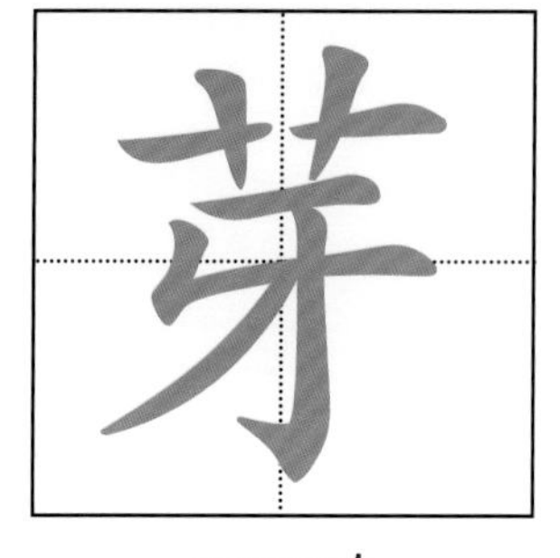

sprout

Word Formation.
字的構成。

kè

客

guest

jiá

夾

clip

é

額

forehead

jiá

頰

cheeks

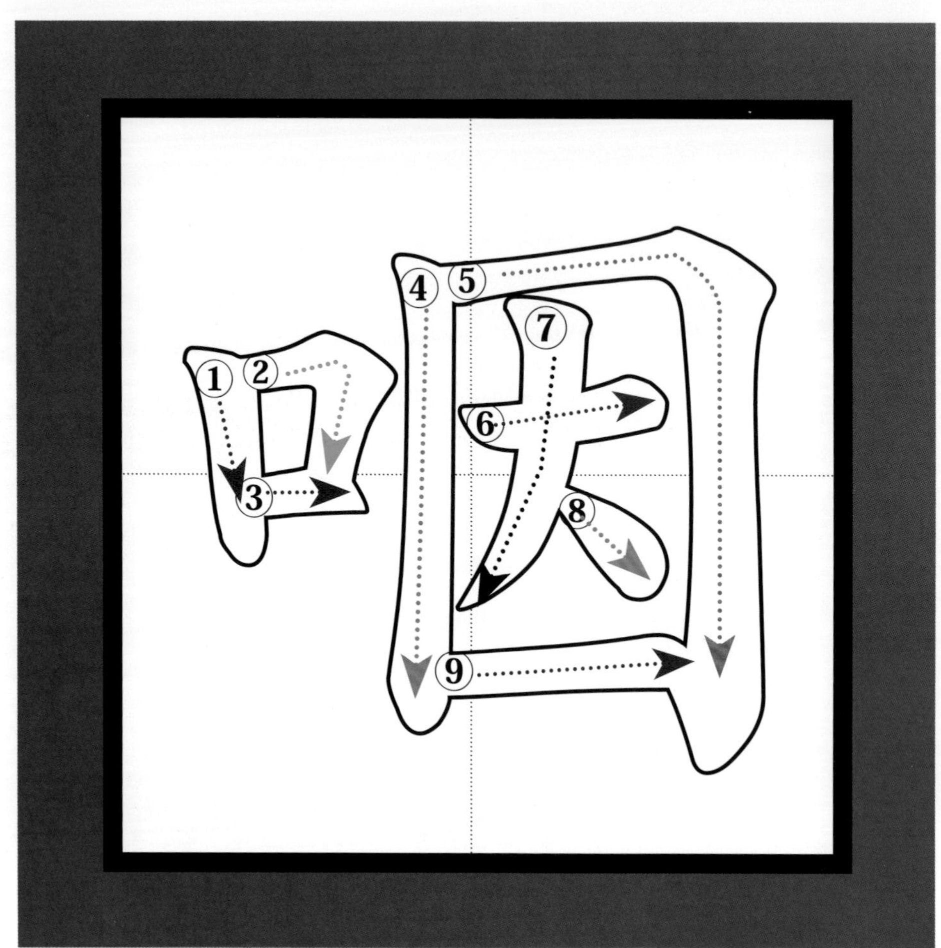
1
2
3
4
5
6
7
8
9

Lesson Three 第三課

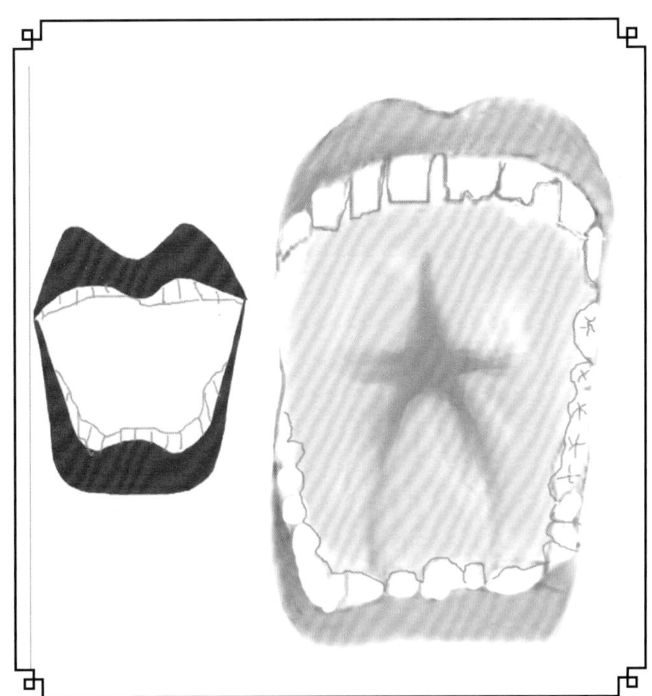

yān

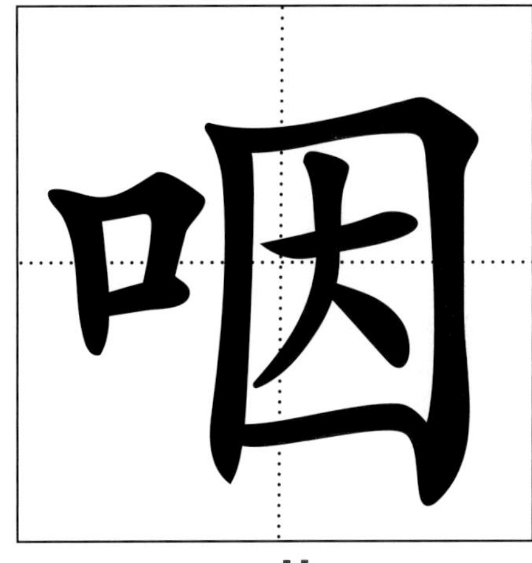

swallow

yān	hóu
咽	喉

throat

1
2
3
4
5
6
7
8
9
10
11
12
13
14
15
16
17

liǎn

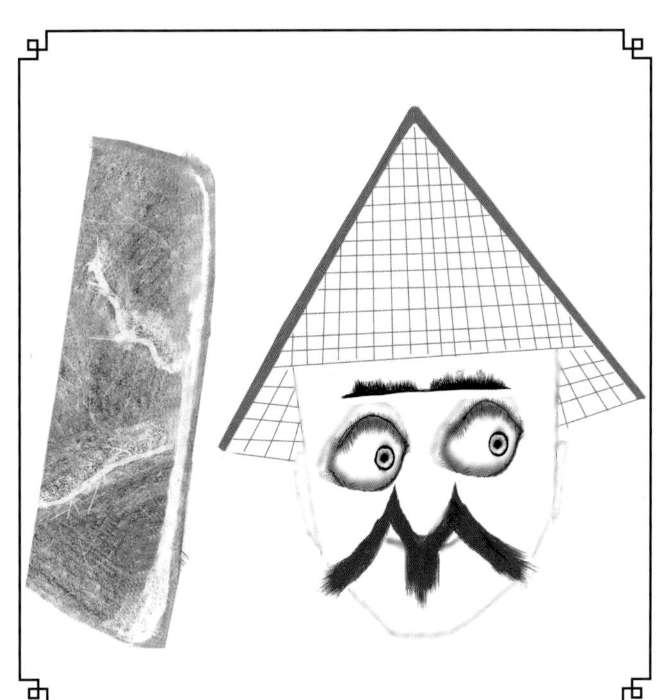

face

liǎn	jiá
臉	頰

cheeks

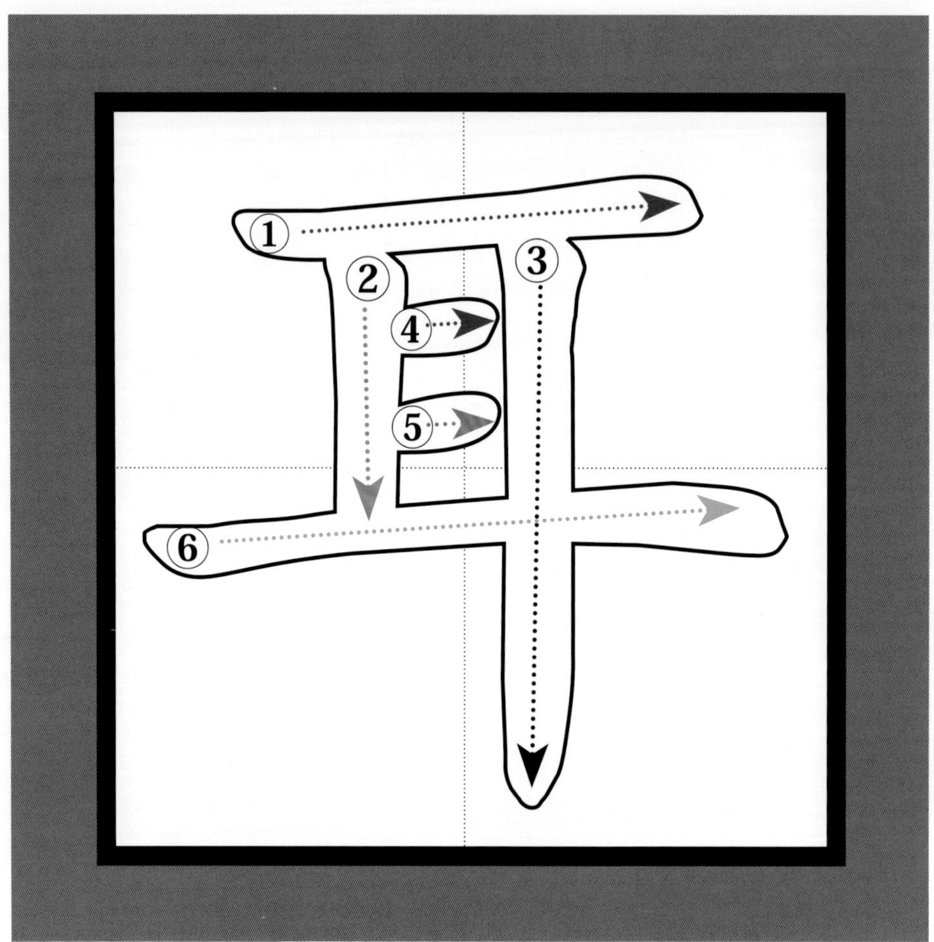
1
2
3
4
5
6

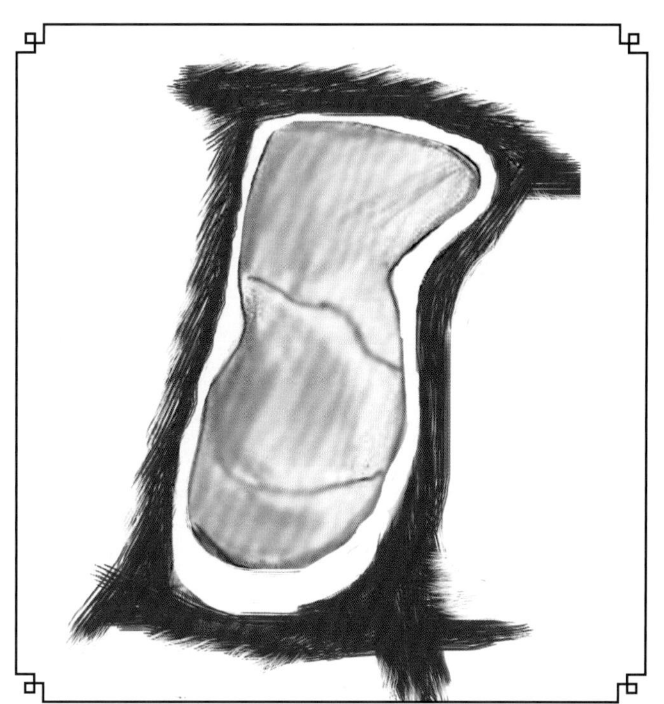

ěr

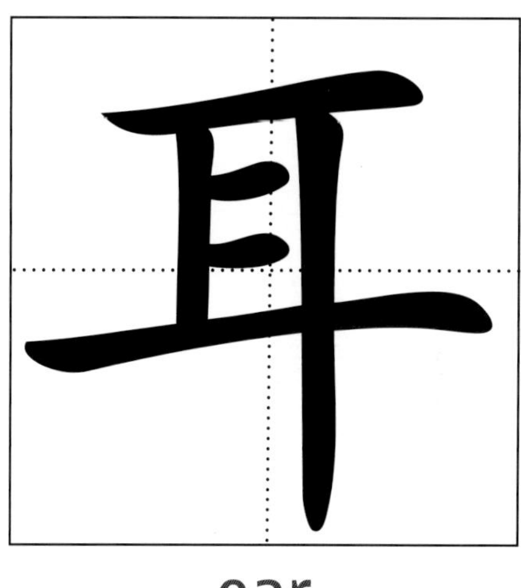

ear

ěr	duo
耳	朵

ear

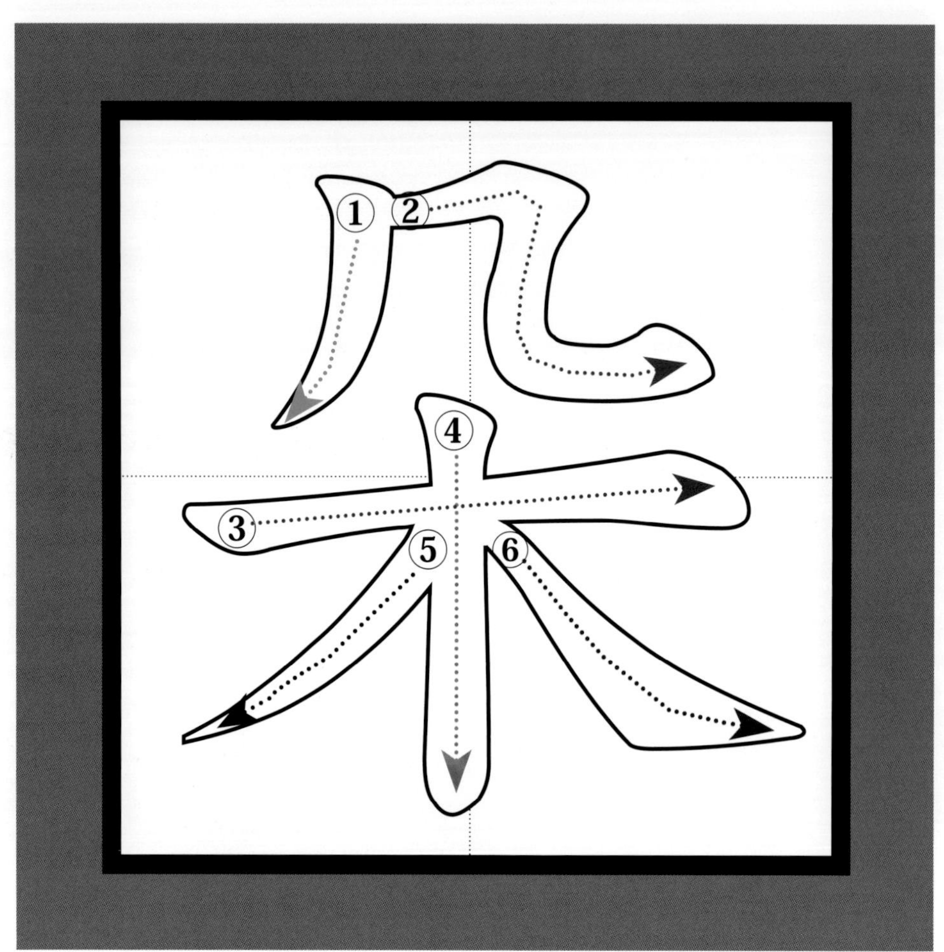
1
2
3
4
5
6

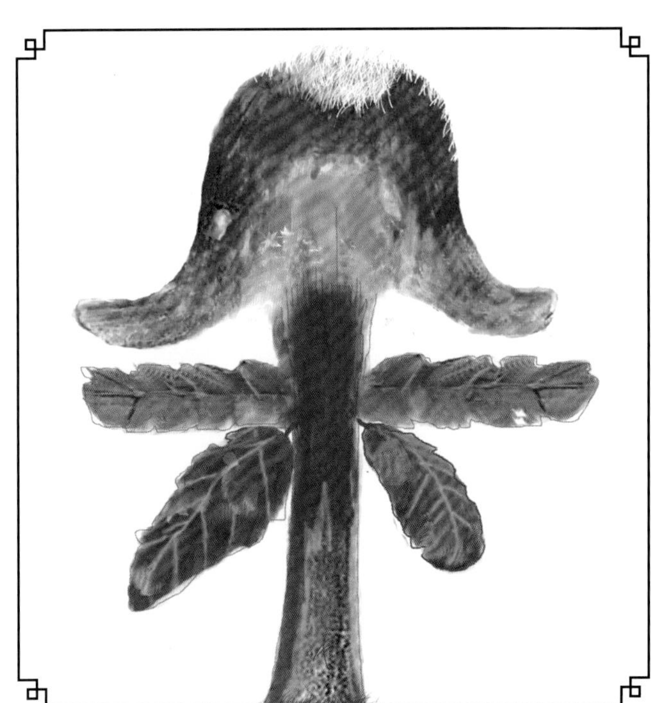

duǒ

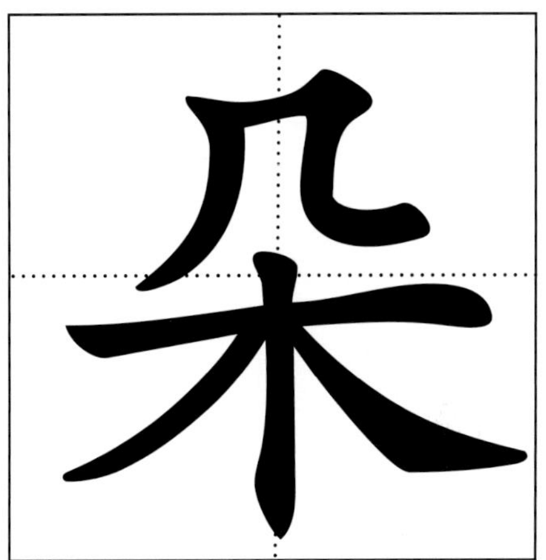

quantifier for flowers

huā	duǒ
花	朵

flowers

1
2
3
4
5
6
7
8
9
10
11
12
13
14
15

fà

hair

hair

Read these words.

讀一讀這些字。

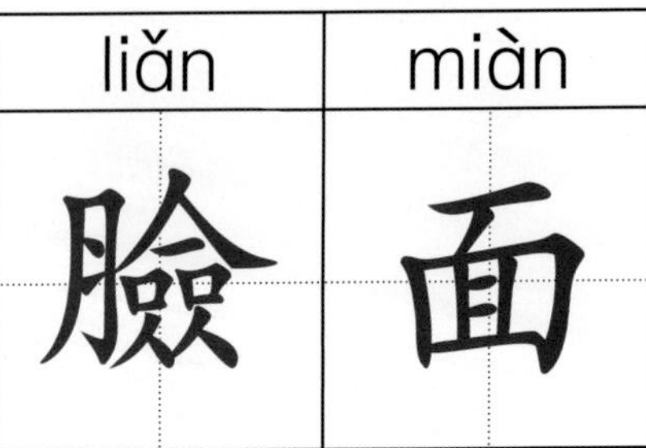

liǎn	miàn
臉	面

face/reputation

bí	kǒng
鼻	孔

nostril

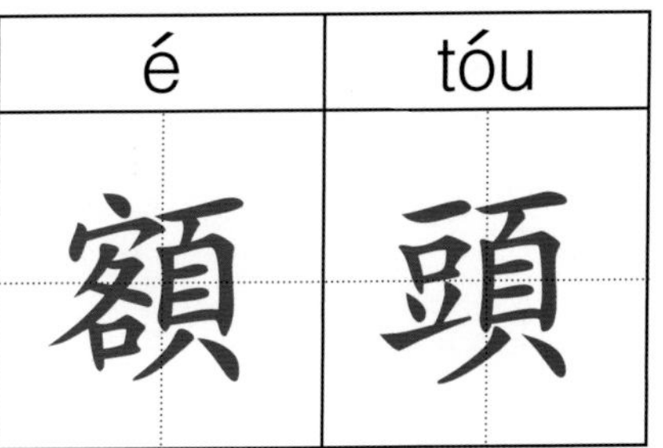

é	tóu
額	頭

forehead

kǒu	shuǐ
口	水

saliva

What do we feel with?
用甚麼感覺事物？

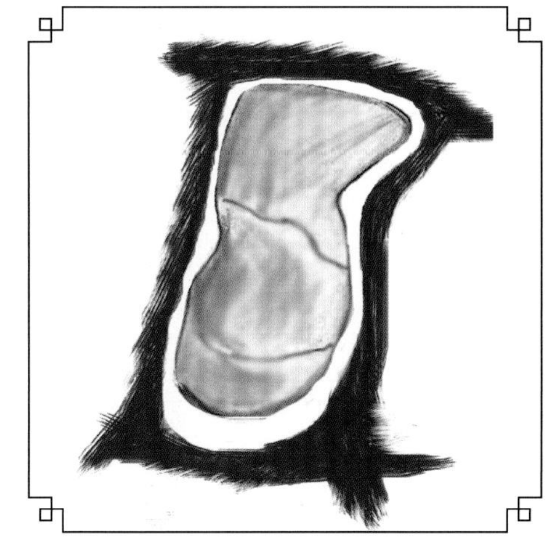

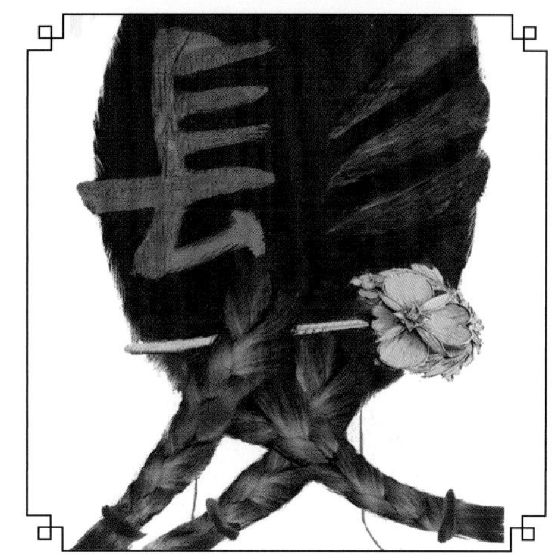

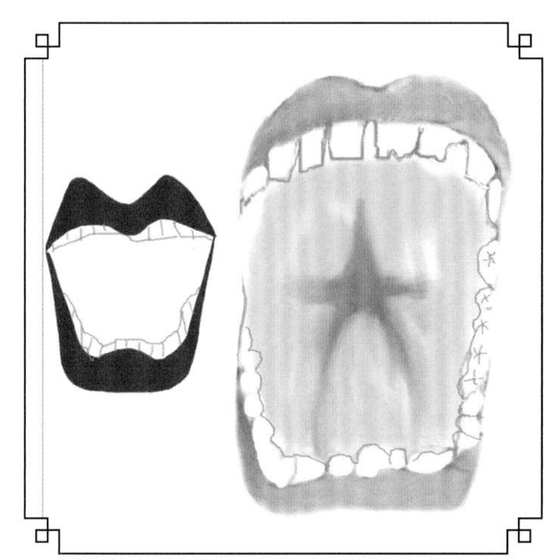

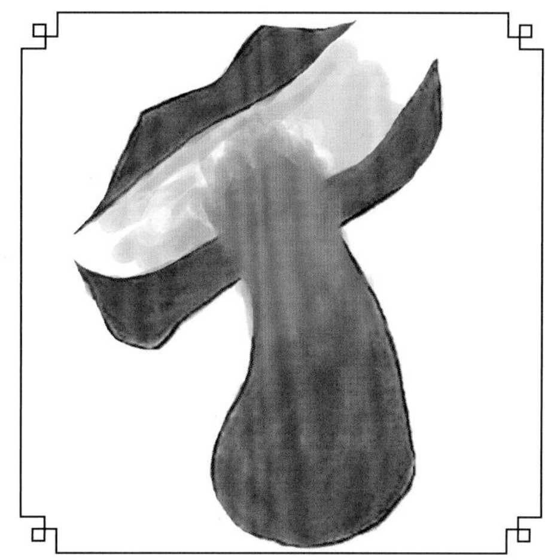

髮耳舌咽

1
2
3
4

shǒu

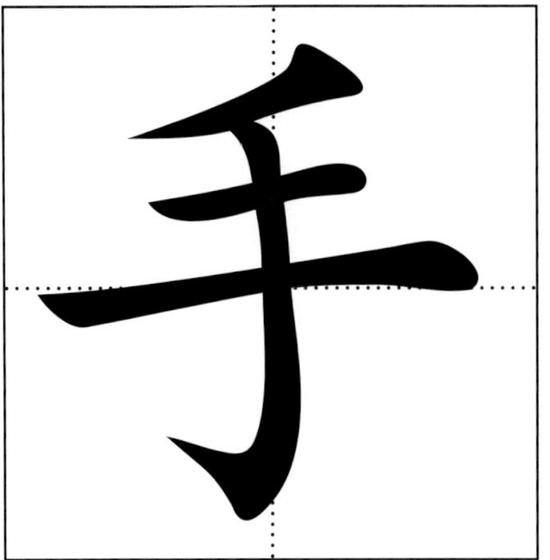

hand

shǒu	zhǐ
手	指

finger

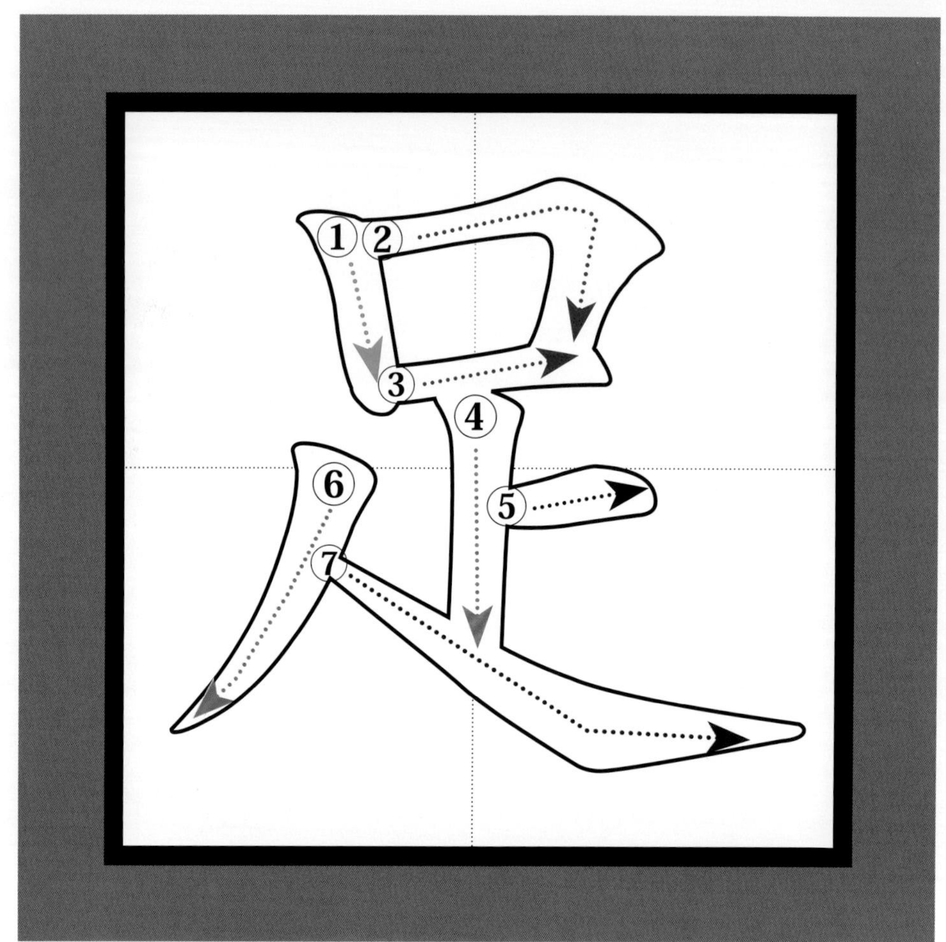
1
2
3
4
5
6
7

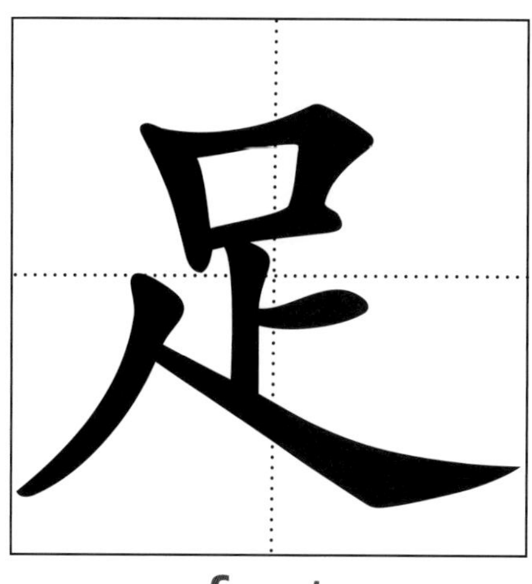

foot

shǒu	zú
手	足

siblings

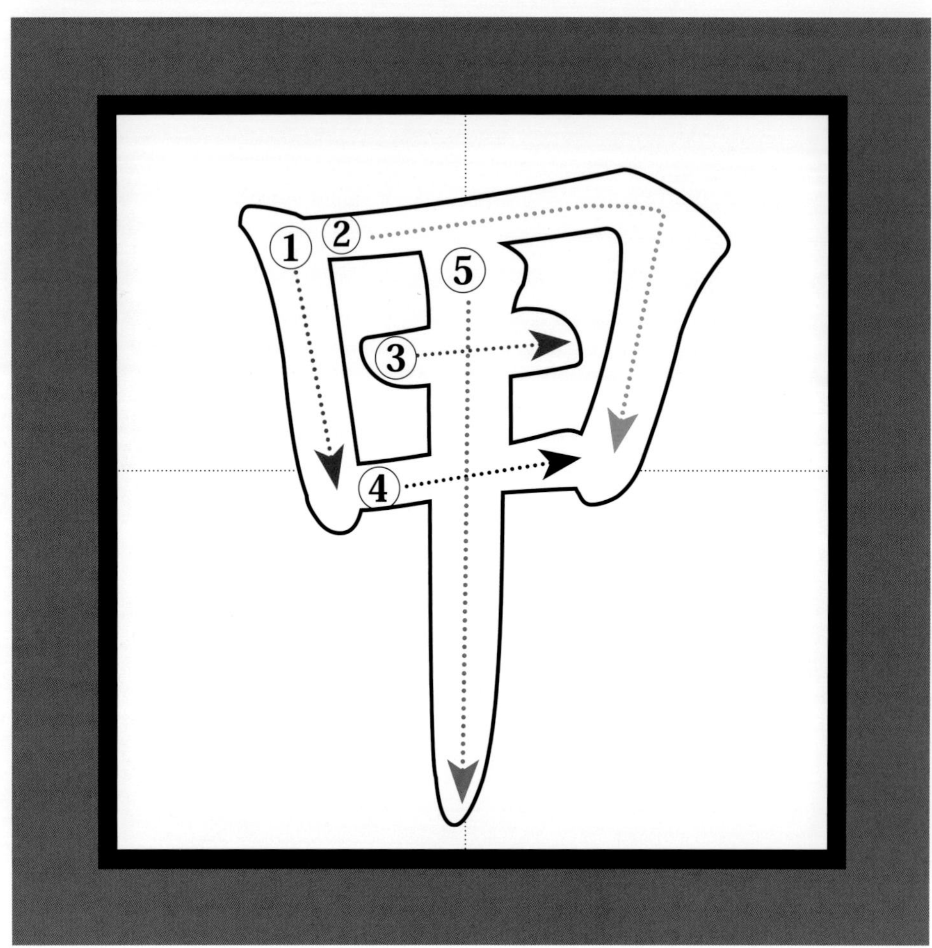
1
2
3
4
5

jiǎ

甲

nail/armor/first

zhǐ	jia
指	甲

finger nails

1
2
3
4
5
6
7
8
9
10
11
12

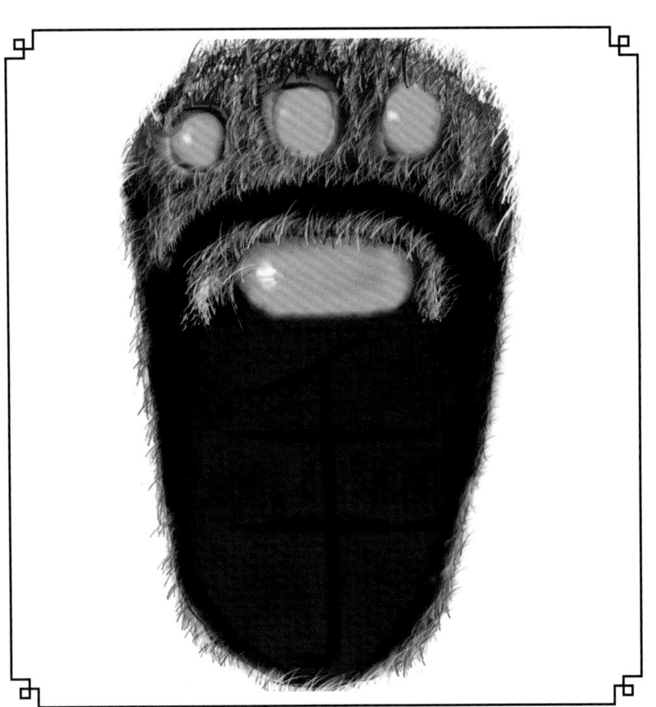

zhǎng

palm/sole/paw

jiǎo	zhǎng
腳	掌

sole

1
2
3
4
5
6
7
8
9
10
11
12
13

jiǎo

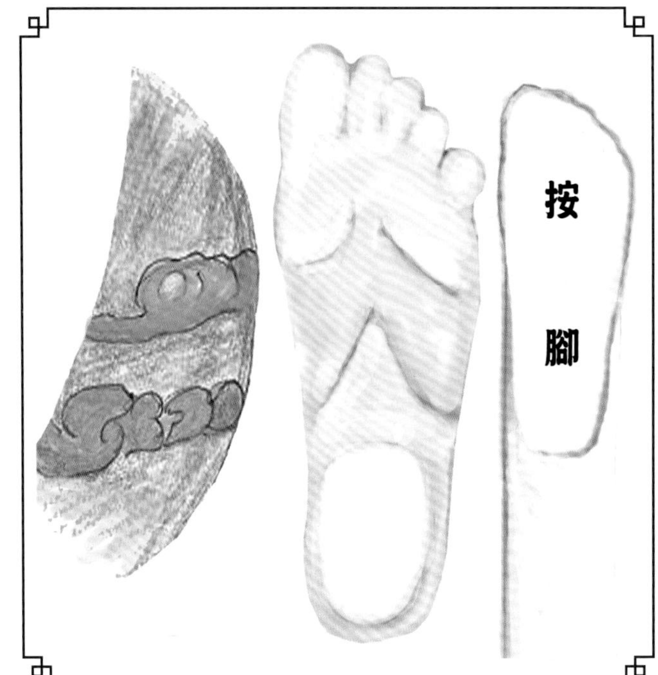

腳

feet

jiǎo	dǐ
腳	底

sole

Word Formation.
字的構成。

			wèi
田	月	=	胃
			stomach

	shì		fèi
月	市	=	肺
	city		lung

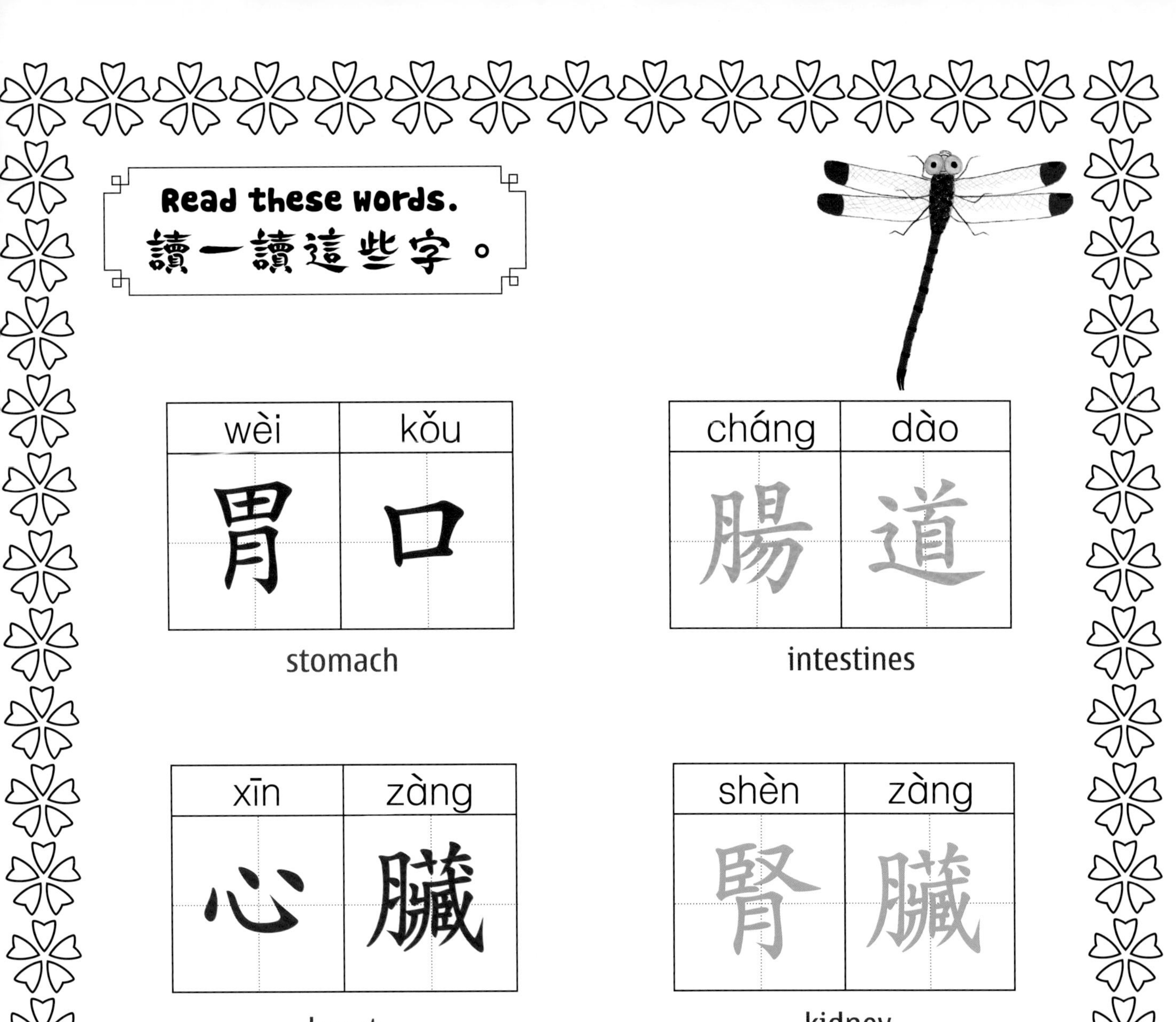

Read these words.
讀一讀這些字。

wèi	kǒu
胃	口

stomach

cháng	dào
腸	道

intestines

xīn	zàng
心	臟

heart

shèn	zàng
腎	臟

kidney

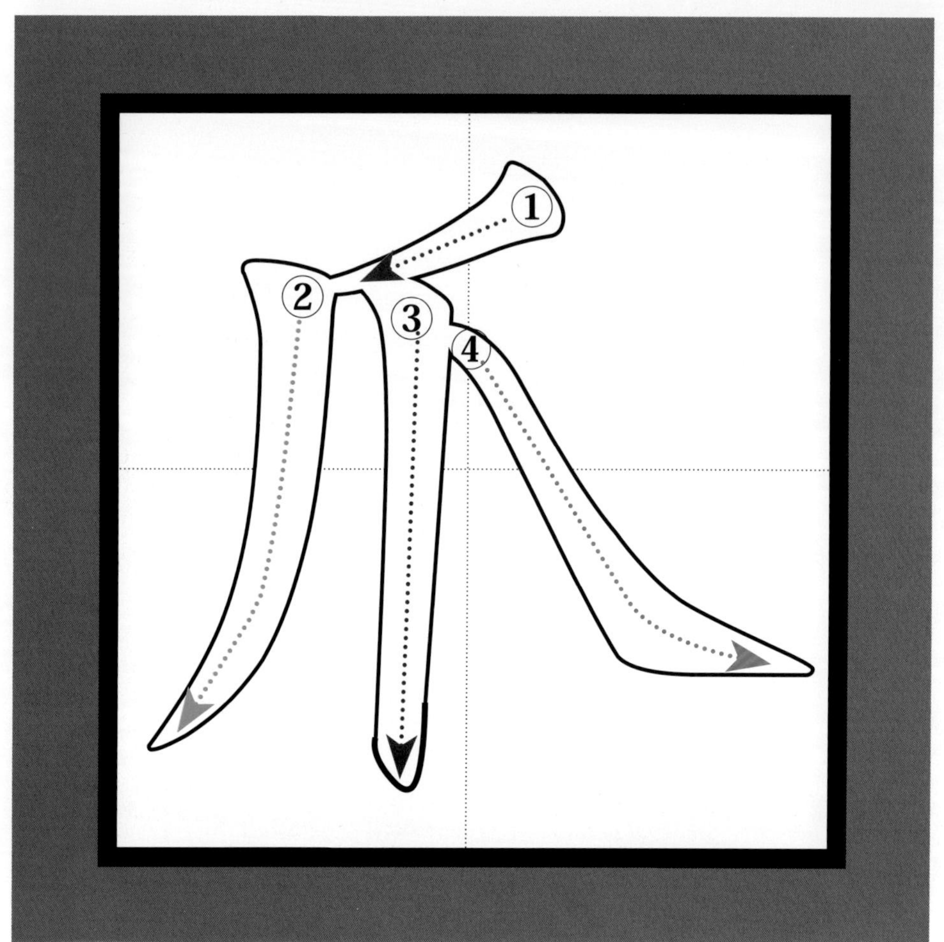
1
2
3
4

Lesson Four 第四課

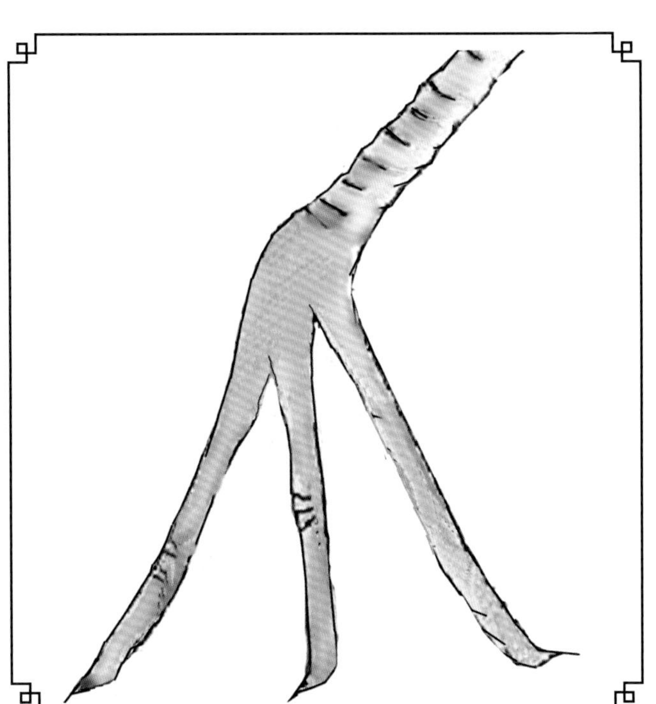

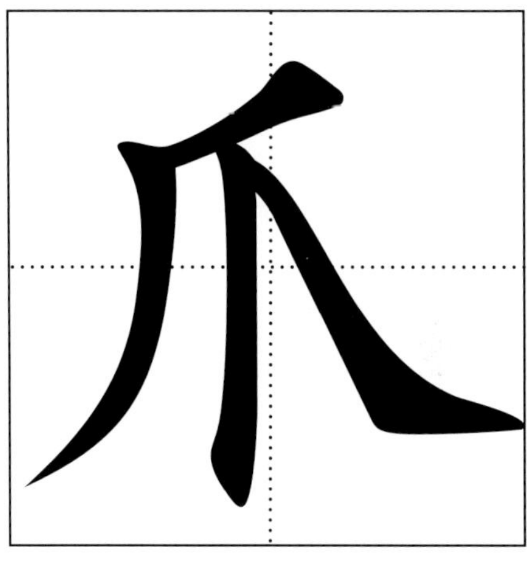

claw

zhuǎ	zi
爪	子

claw/paw

1
2
3
4
5
6
7
8

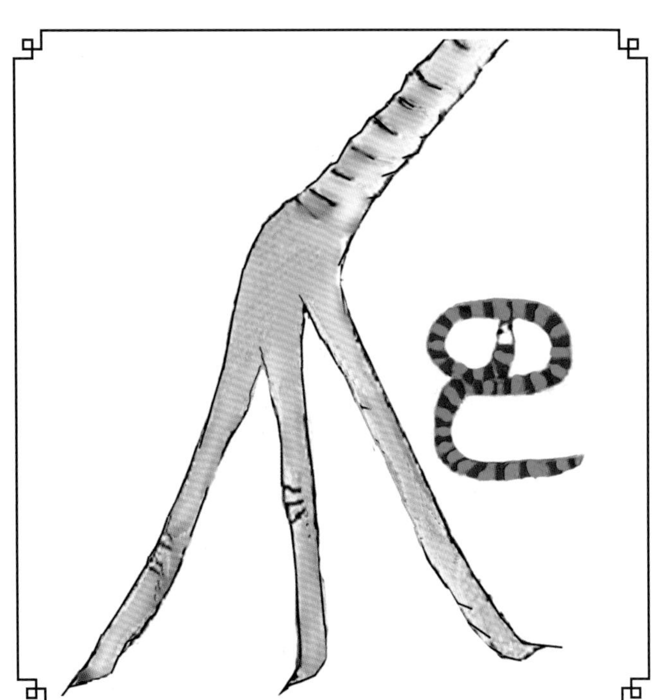

pá

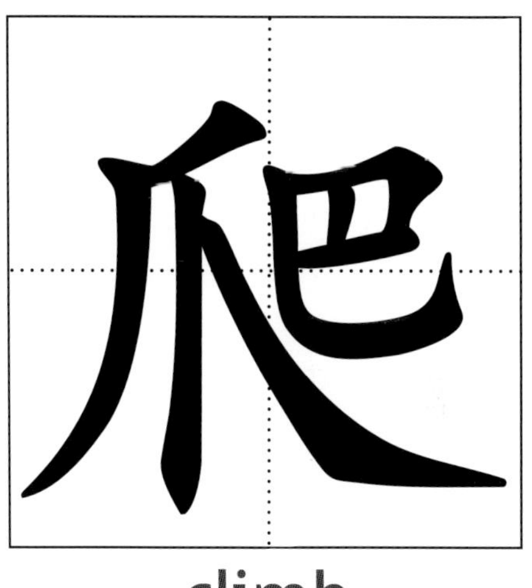

climb

pá	shān
爬	山

climbing mountain

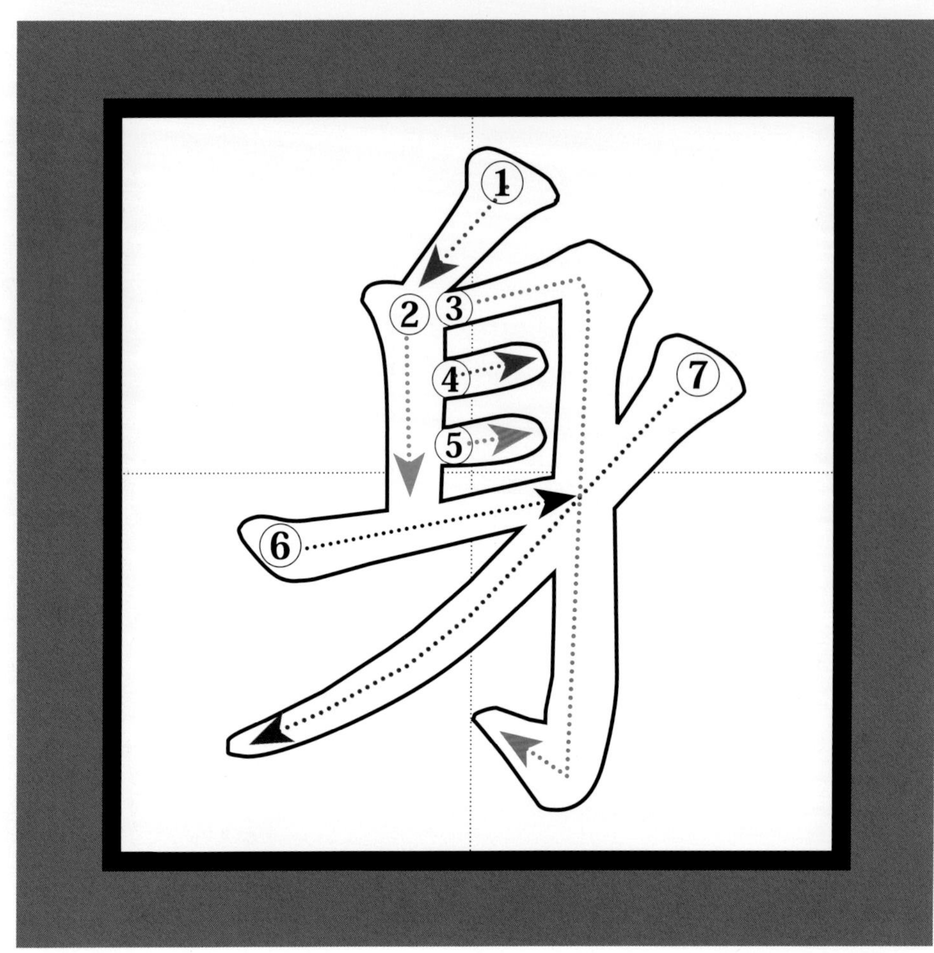

1
2
3
4
5
6
7

shēn

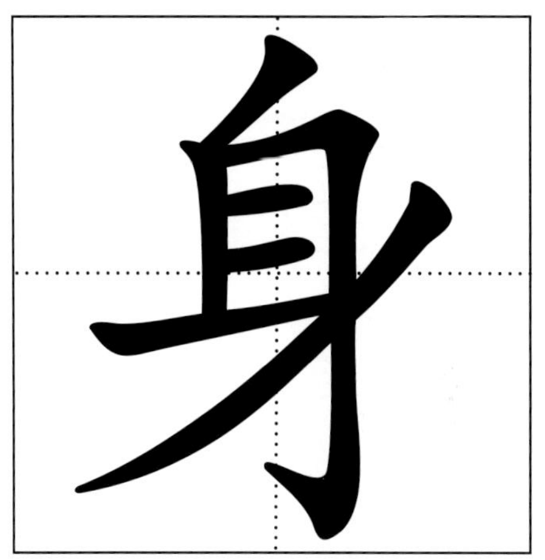

body

shēn	tǐ
身	體

body

1
2
3
4
5
6
7
8
9

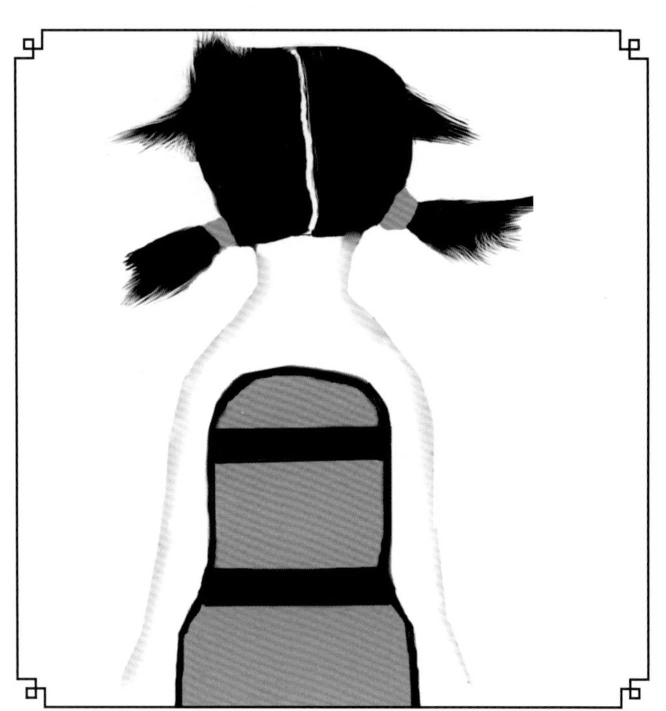

bèi

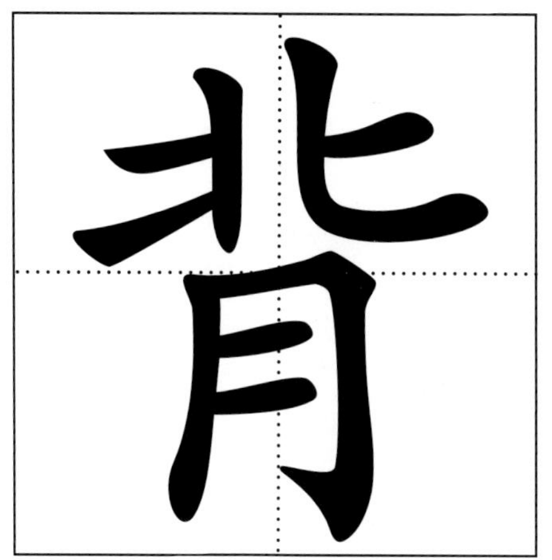

back

hòu	bèi
後	背

back

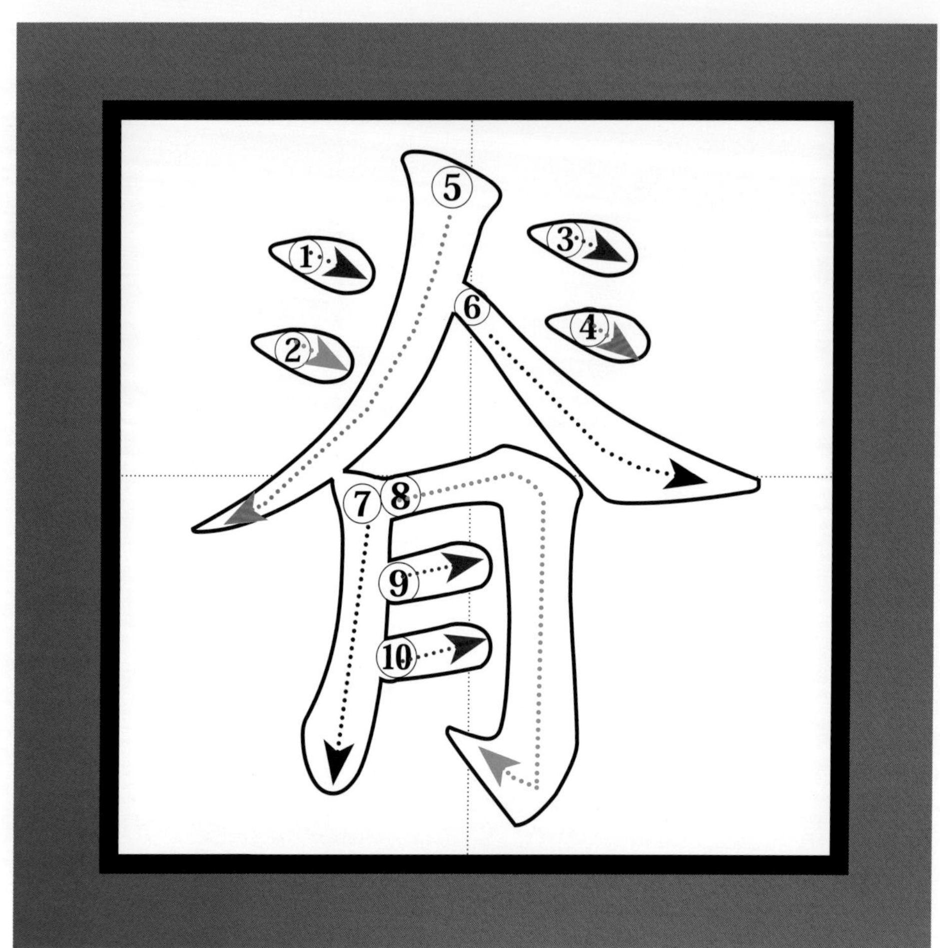
1
2
3
4
5
6
7
8
9
10

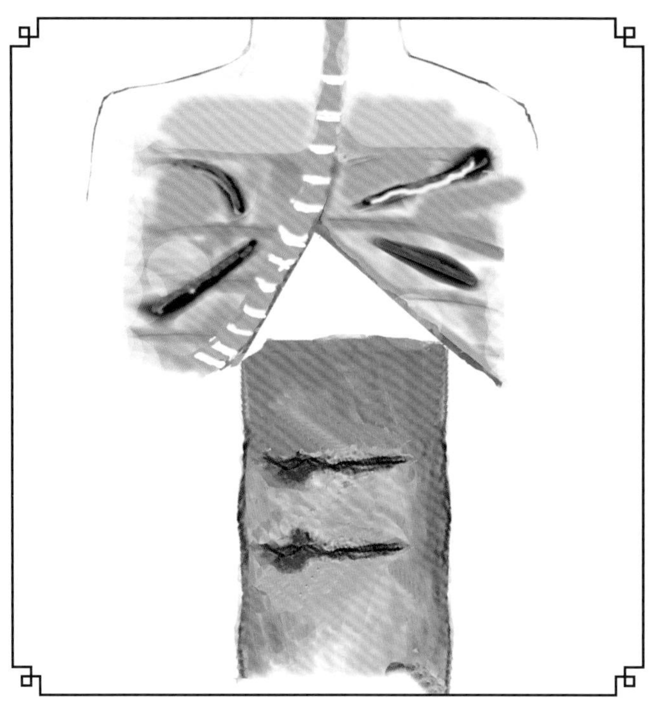

jǐ

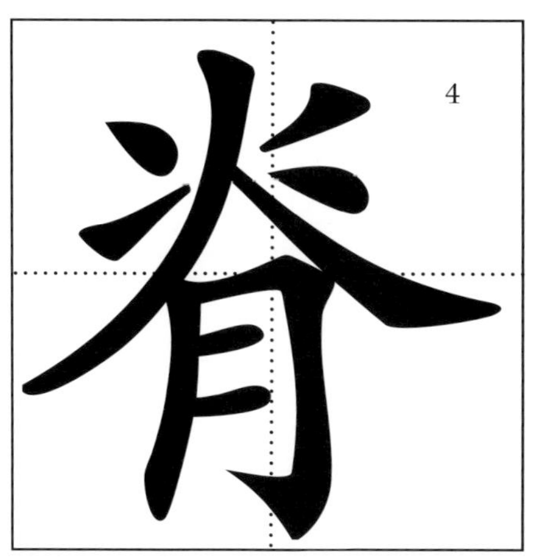

spine

jǐ	zhuī
脊	椎

spine

4. The strokes of this word may appear to be different in different fonts. 這個字的不同字體筆畫表現得有些不同。

Read these words.
讀一讀這些字。

the back of a hand

behind

jiǎo	zhǐ
腳	趾

toes

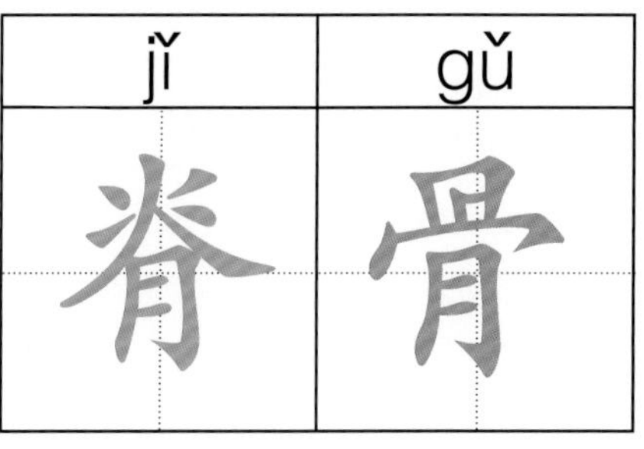

a backbone

Which is the word for human?

哪個字是表示人的？

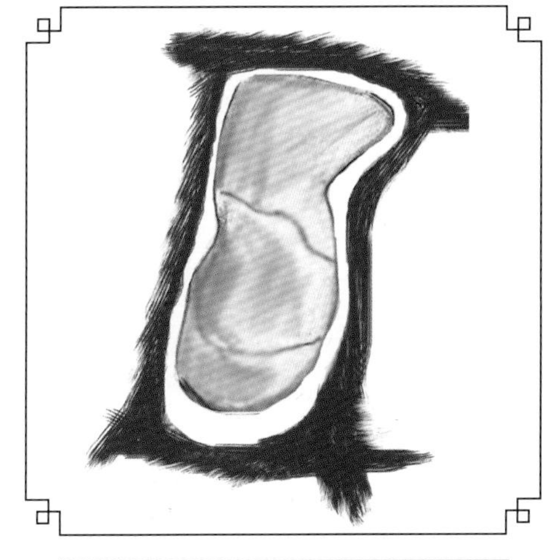

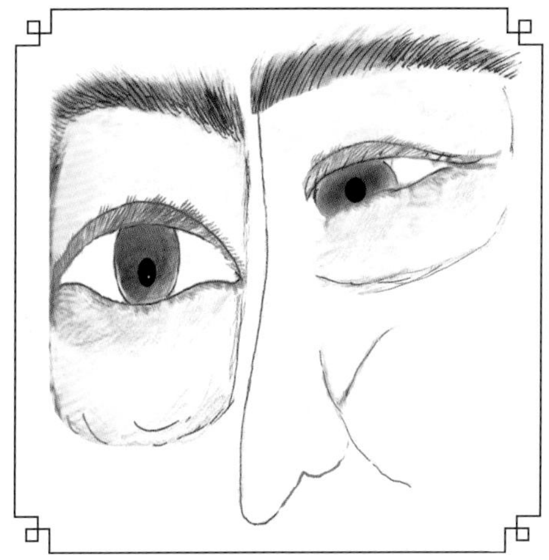

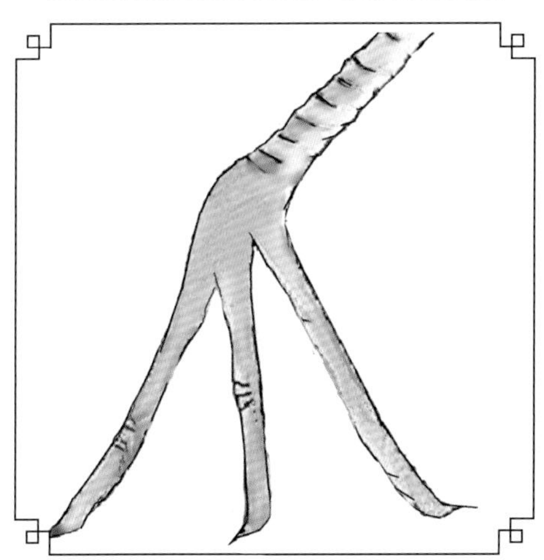

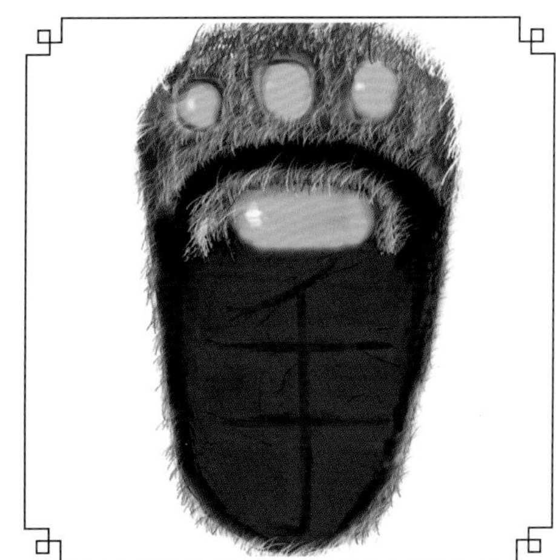

眼爪掌耳

1
2
3
4
5
6
7
8
9
10

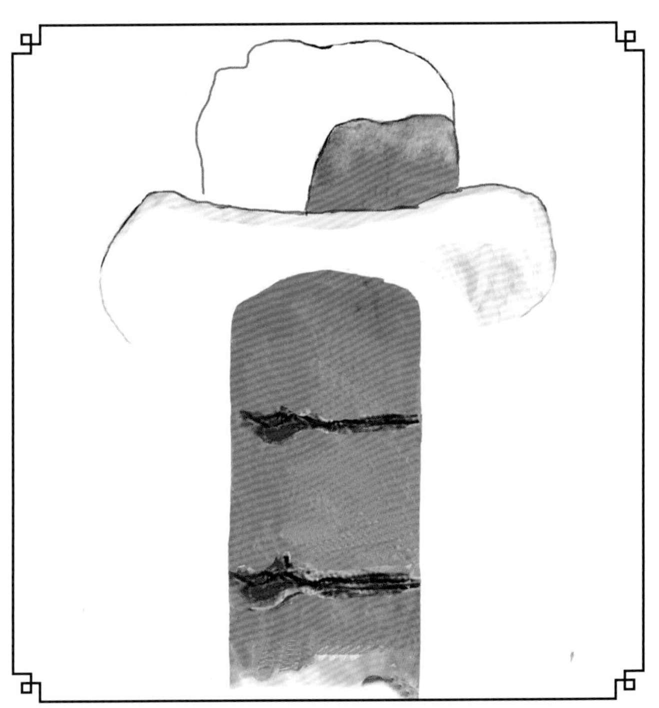

gǔ

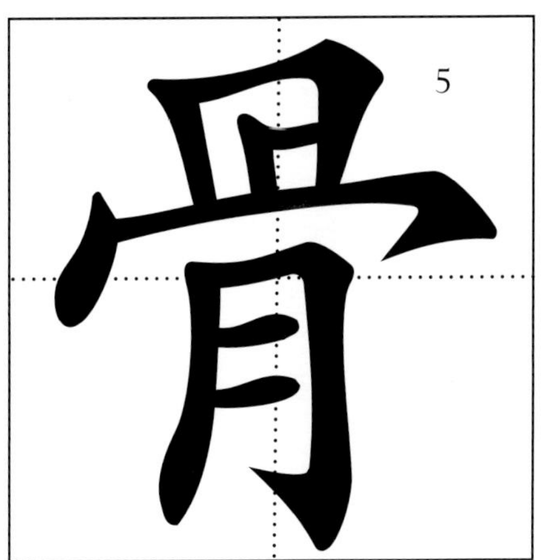

bone

gǔ	tou
骨	頭

bone

5. The strokes of this word may appear to be different in different fonts. 這個字的不同字體筆畫表現得有些不同。

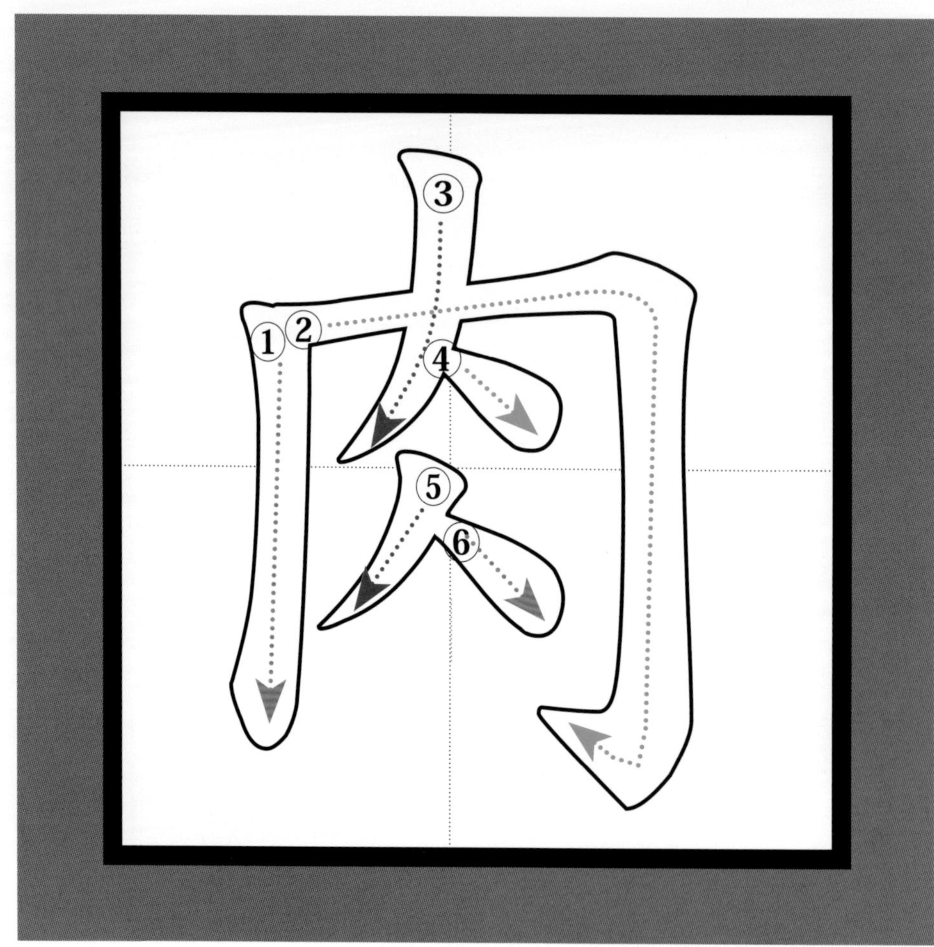
1
2
3
4
5
6

rròu

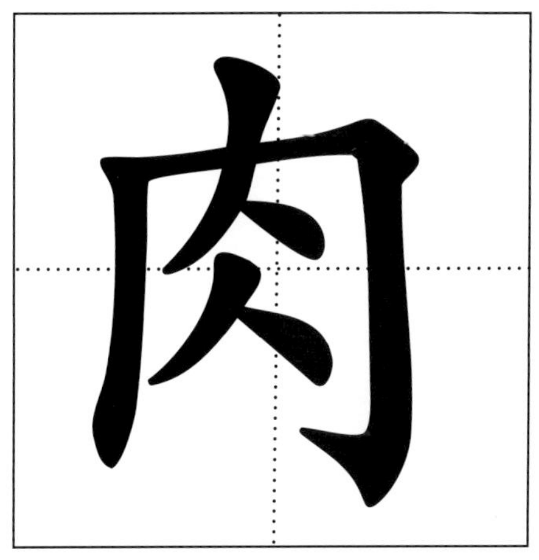

meat

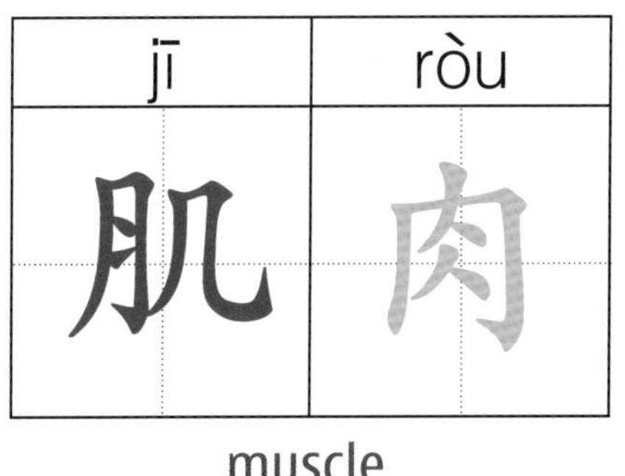

muscle

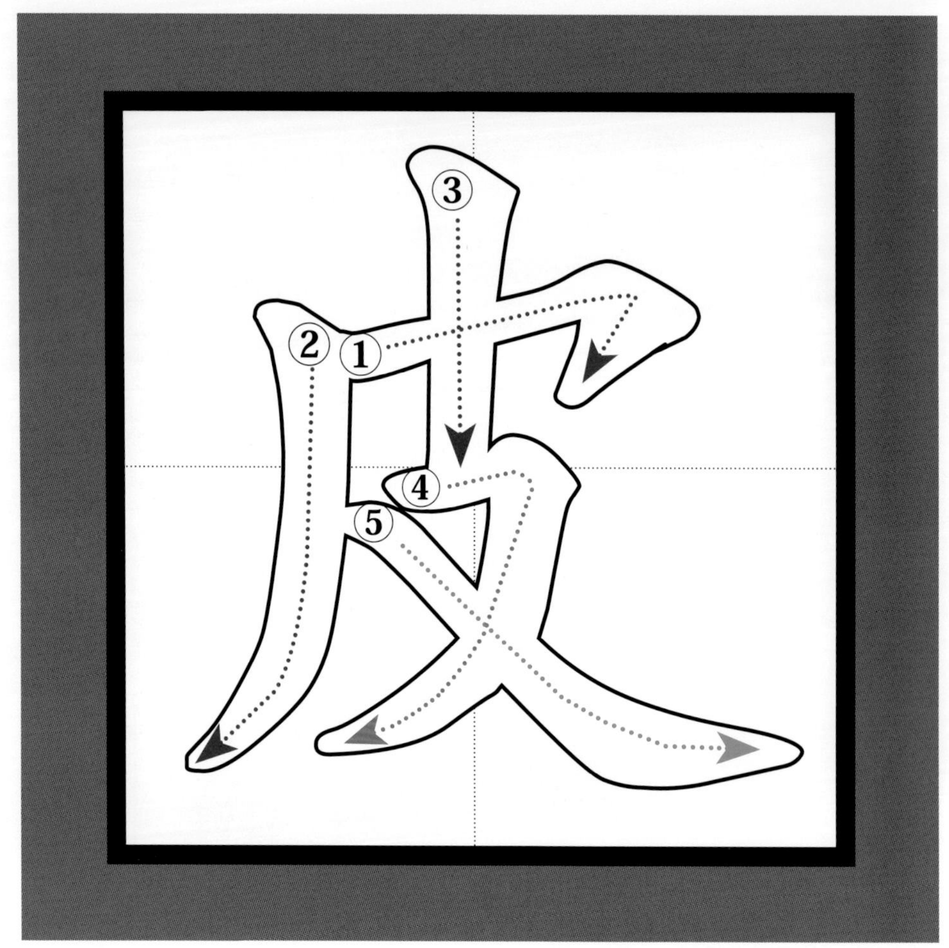

1
2
3
4
5

pí

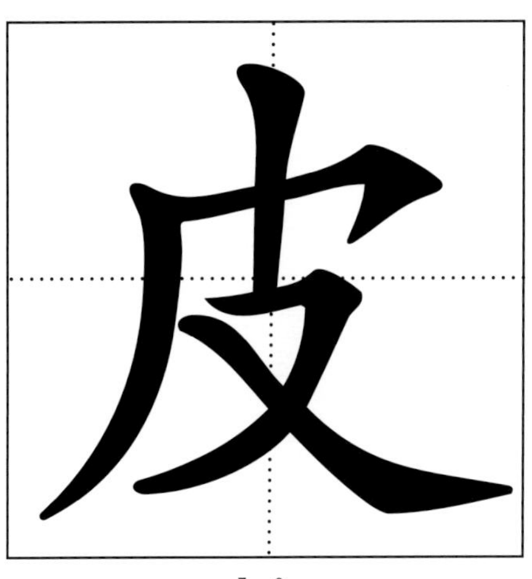

skin

shù	pí
樹	皮

bark

1
2
3
4
5
6

xuè

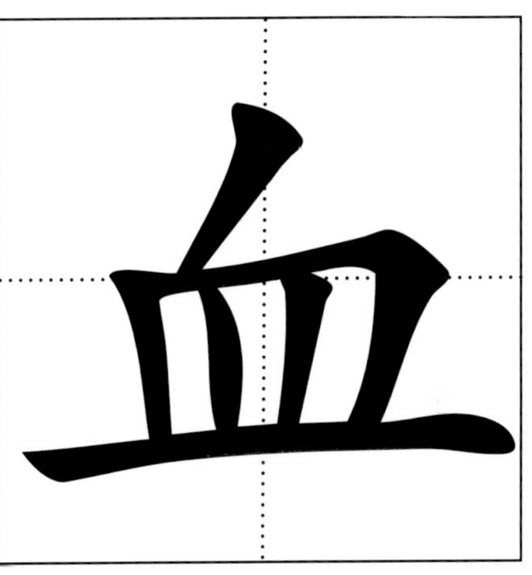

blood

xuè	guǎn
血	管

blood vessel

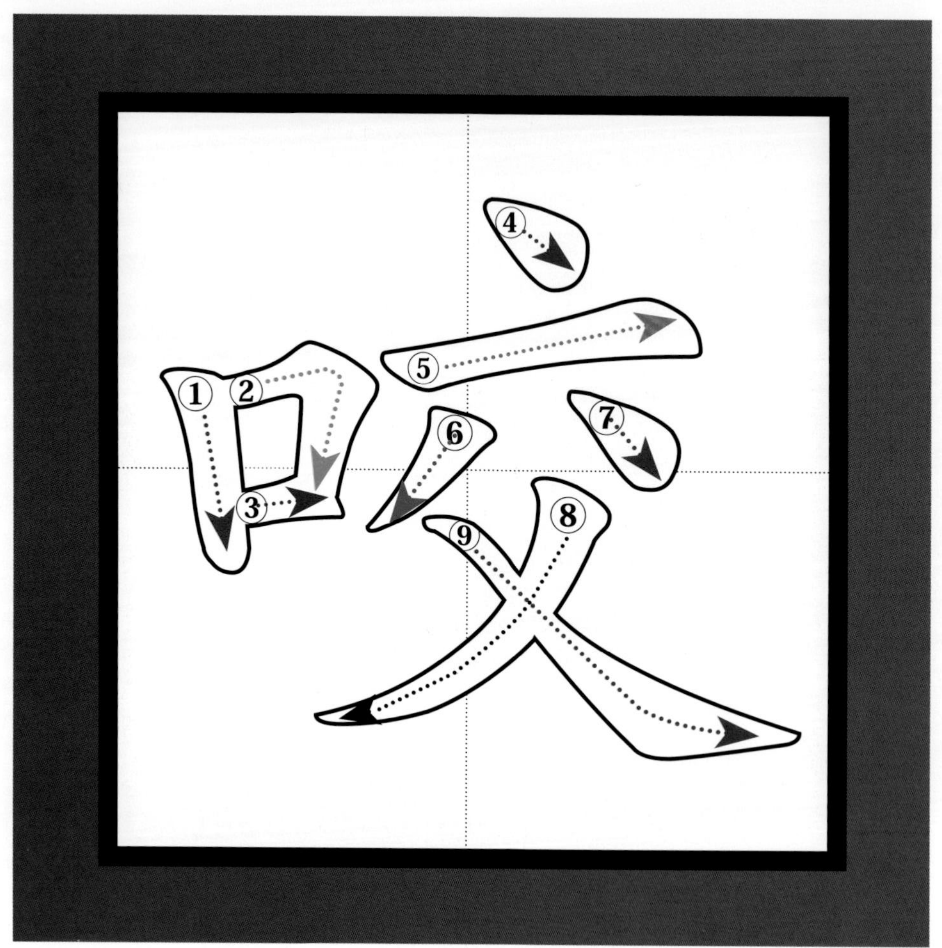
1
2
3
4
5
6
7
8
9

yǎo

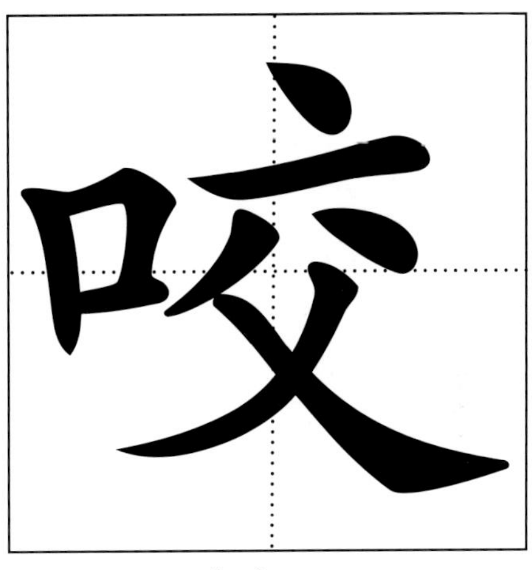

bite

yǎo	rén
咬	人

biting

Read these words.
讀一讀這些字。

gǔ	ròu
骨	肉

relatives

pí	máo
皮	毛

fur

xuè	yè
血	液

blood

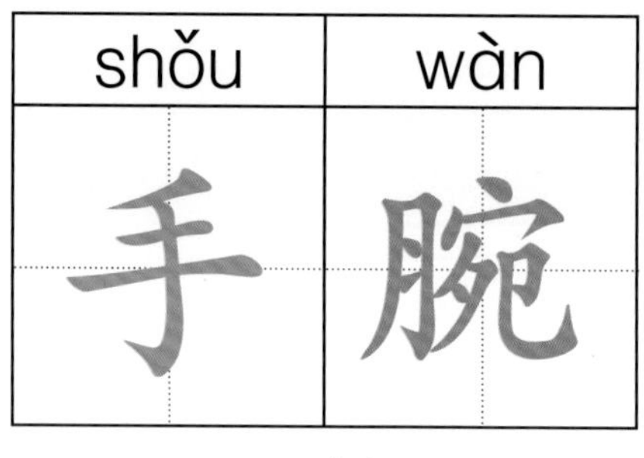

shǒu	wàn
手	腕

wrist

What do you bite things with?

用甚麼咬東西？

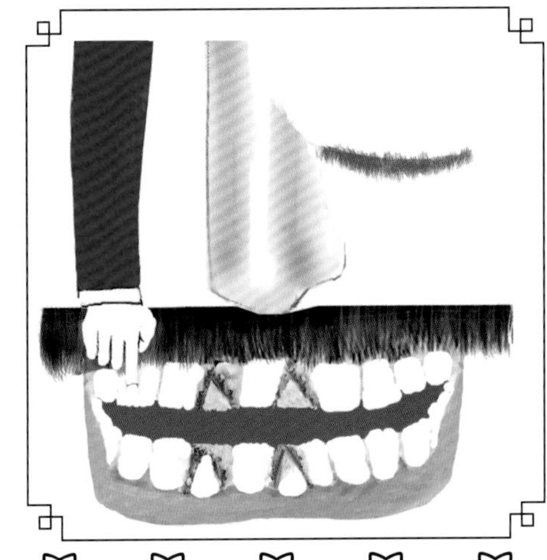

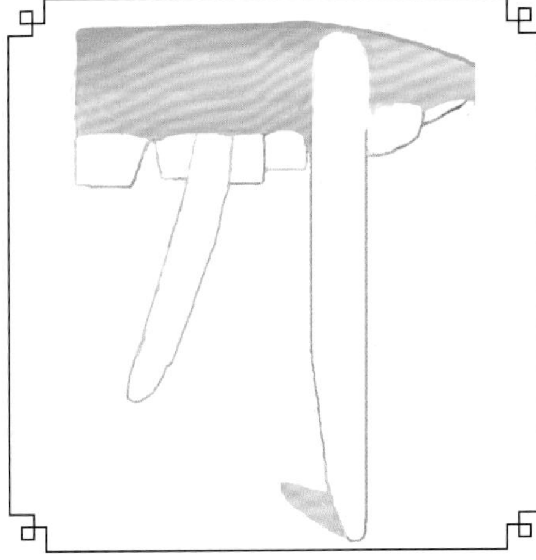

唇牙背齒

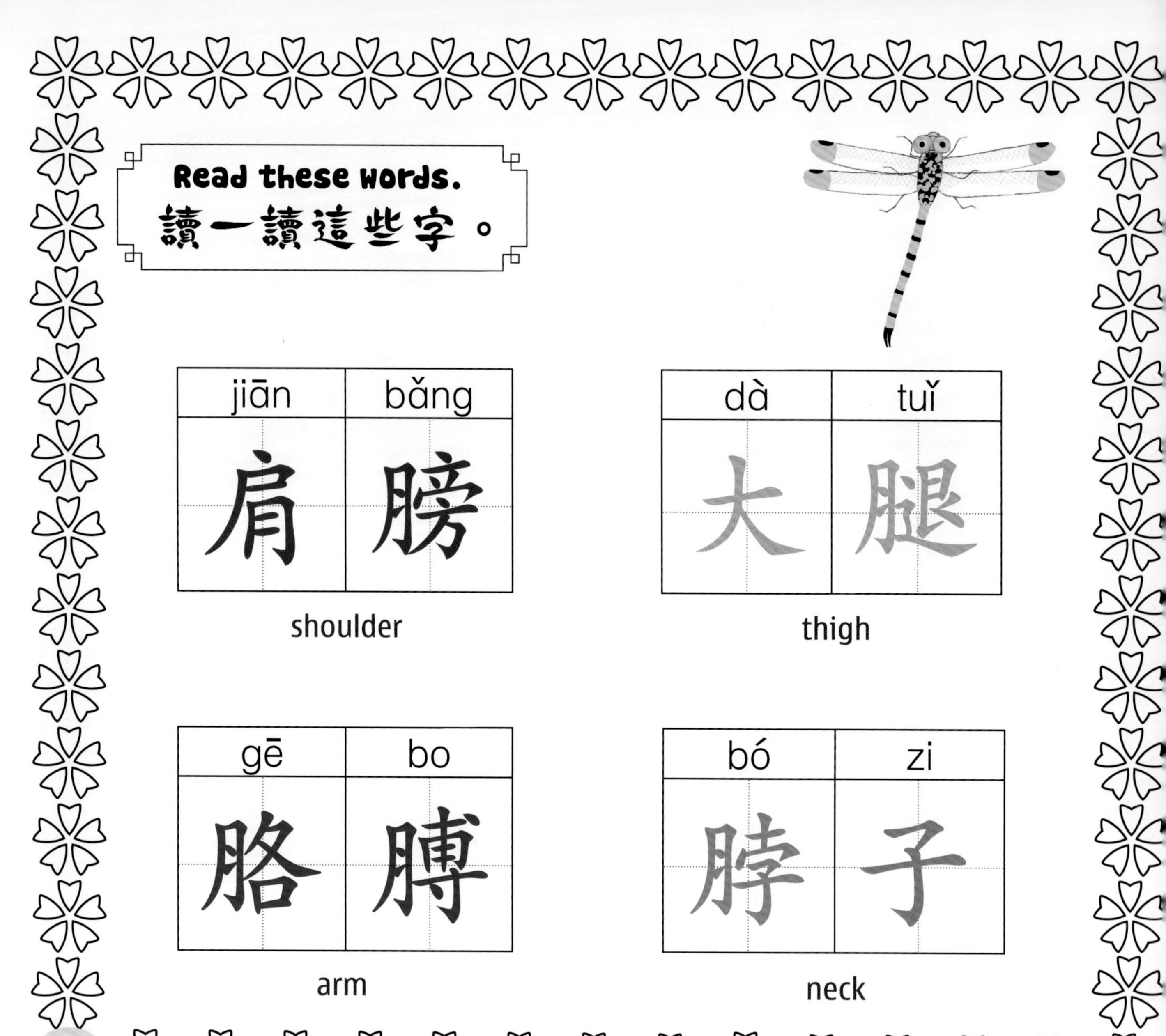

Read these words.

讀一讀這些字。

jiān	bǎng
肩	膀

shoulder

dà	tuǐ
大	腿

thigh

gē	bo
胳	膊

arm

bó	zi
脖	子

neck

Read the following passage.

讀一讀下列短文。

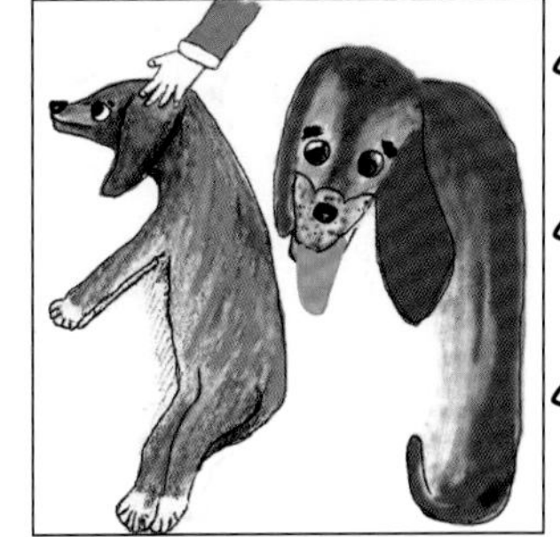

xiǎo gǒu yǒu dà dà de yǎn jing

小狗有大大的眼睛、

The puppy has big eyes,

xiǎo xiǎo de bí zi dà dà de zuǐ ba

小小的鼻子、大大的嘴巴、

a small nose, a big mouth,

sì tiáo tuǐ liǎng zhī ěr duo hé

四條腿、兩隻耳朵和

four legs, two ears and

sì zhī zhuǎ zi xiǎo gǒu shēn shang yǒu máo hé

四隻爪子。小狗身上有毛和

four paws. There is hair on the puppy's body.

wěi ba tā zuì ài chī gǔ tou

尾巴。牠最愛吃骨頭。

It has a tail. The puppy likes eating bones.

Recite the following chant.
背誦下列童謠。

頭、肩膀、膝蓋、腳、
膝蓋、腳。
啊！眼睛、鼻子、
還有口。
頭、肩膀、膝蓋、腳、
膝蓋、腳。

Stickers
小貼紙

Stick the following cartoon stickers on Page 105 to Page 111 to match the Chinese words.
將漢字卡通小貼紙黏貼在 105 頁到 111 頁它們對應的大字上。

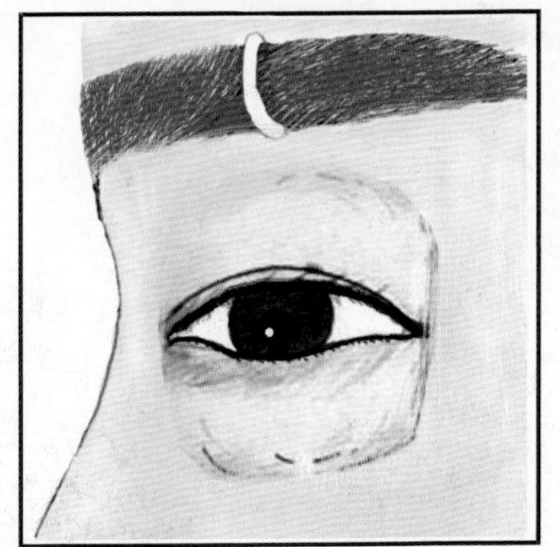

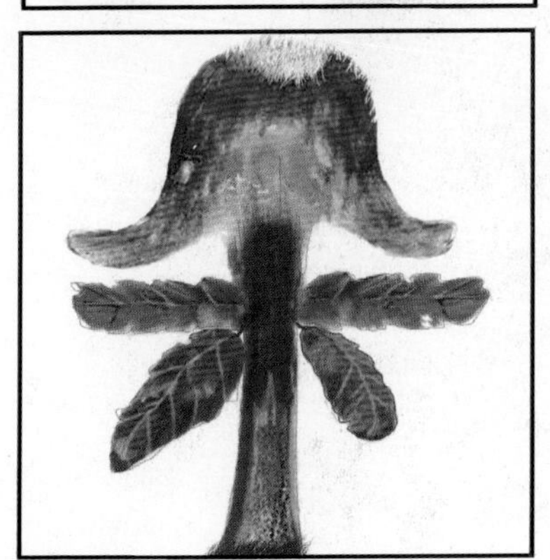
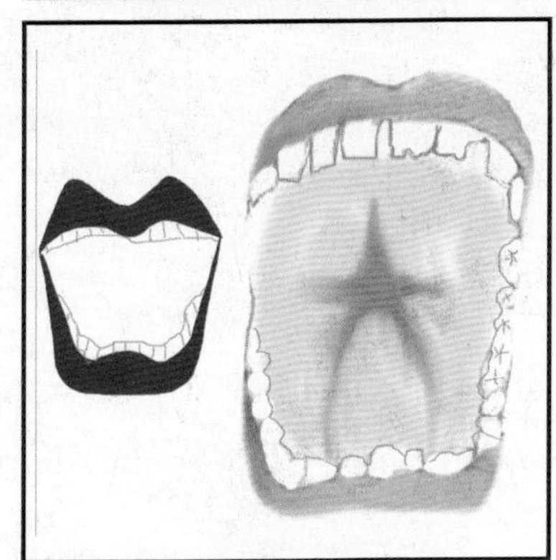

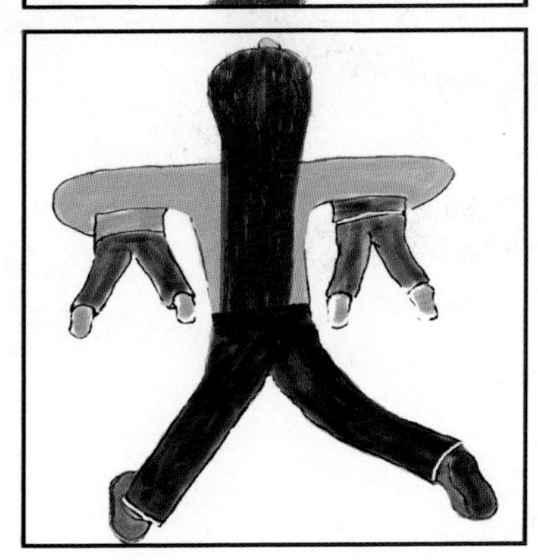
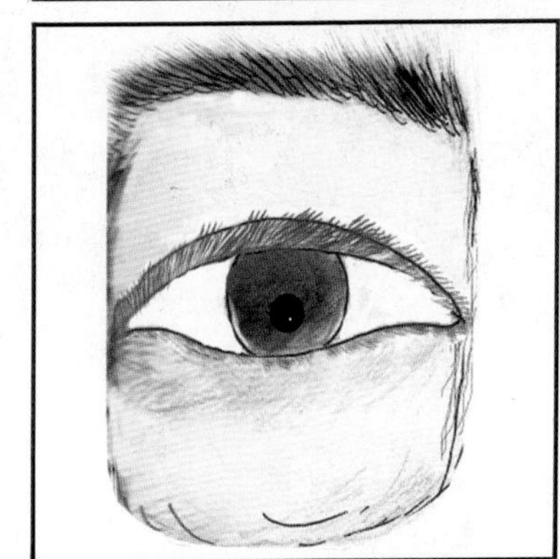
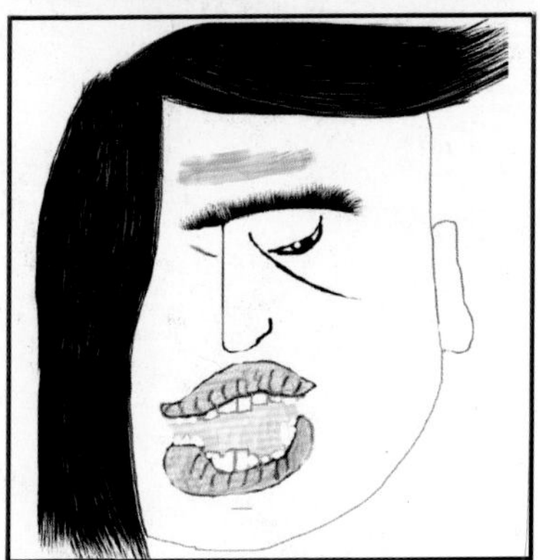

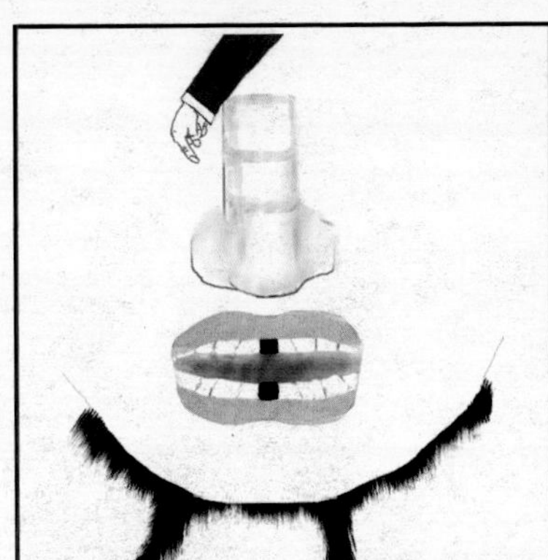
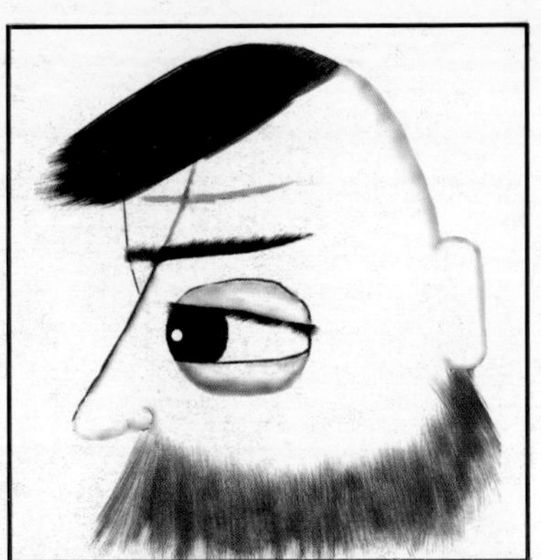
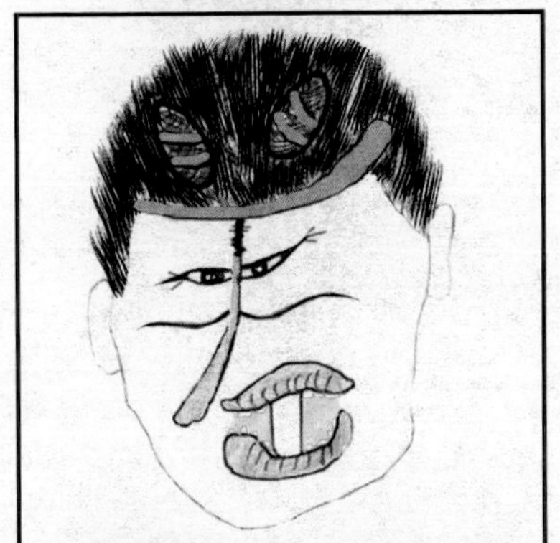
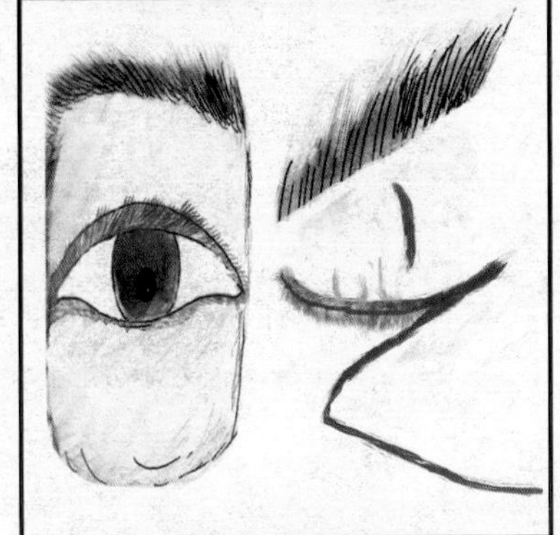
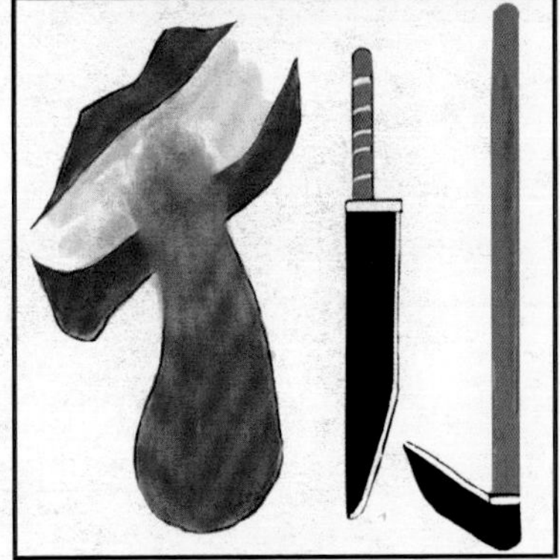
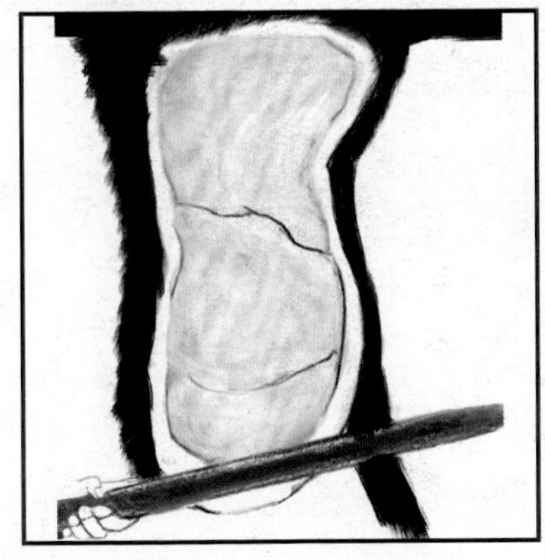

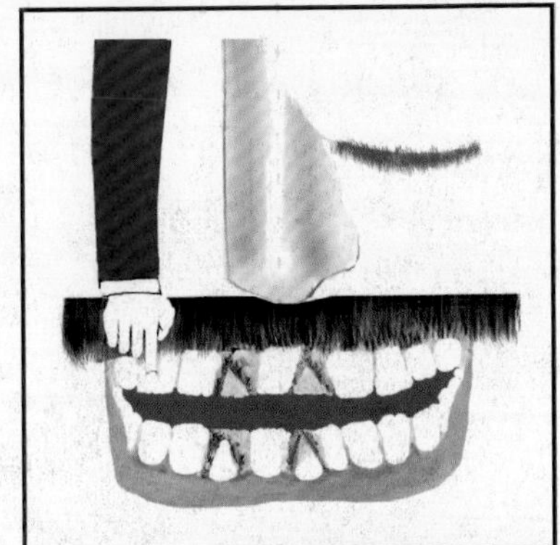
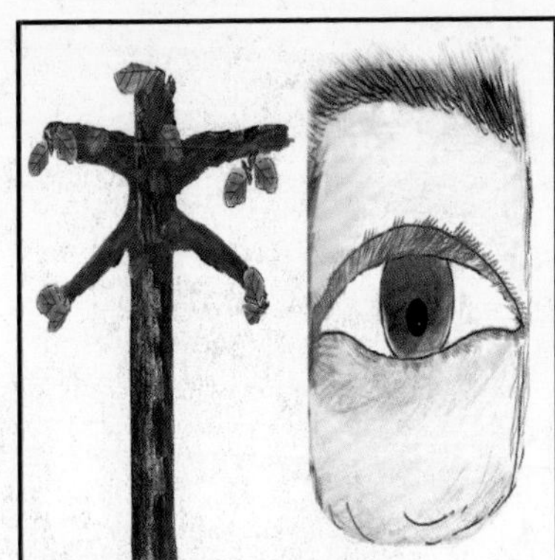
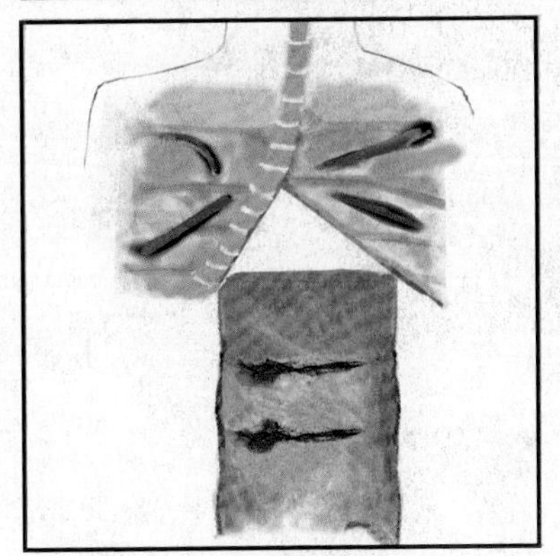
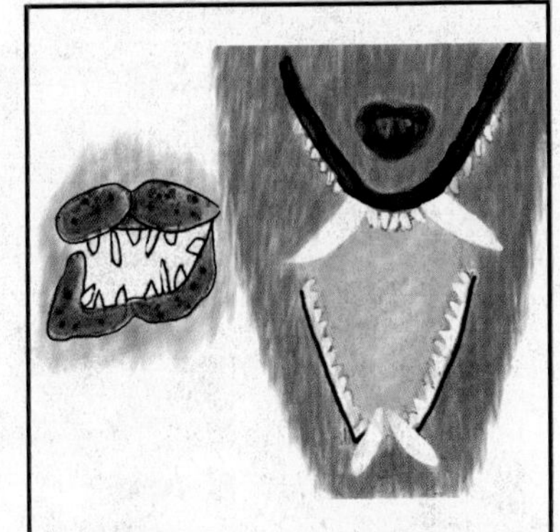

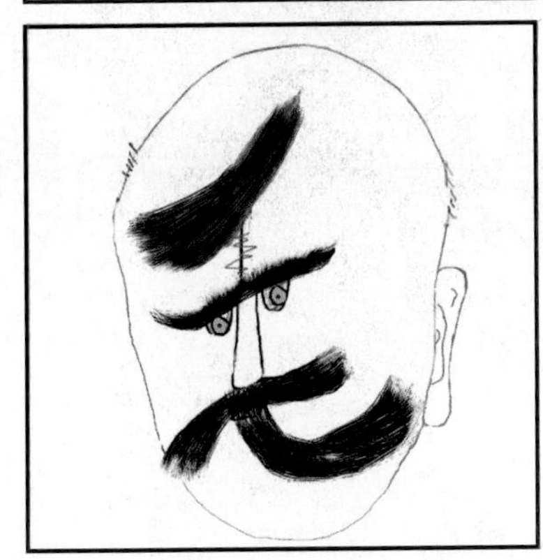
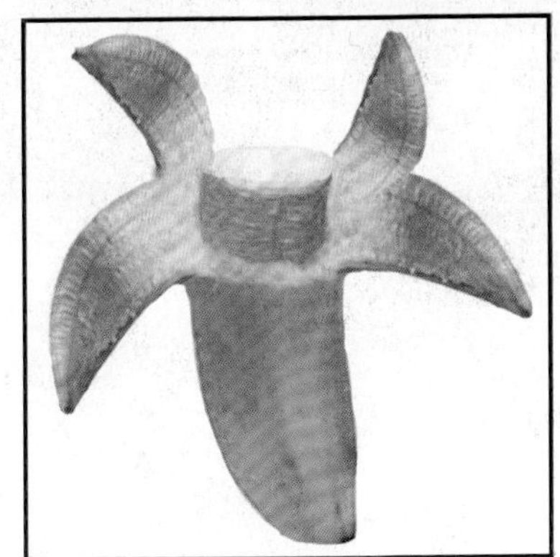
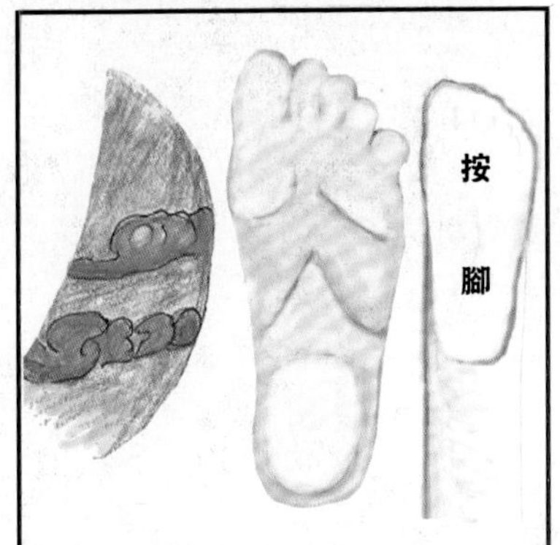
按
腳

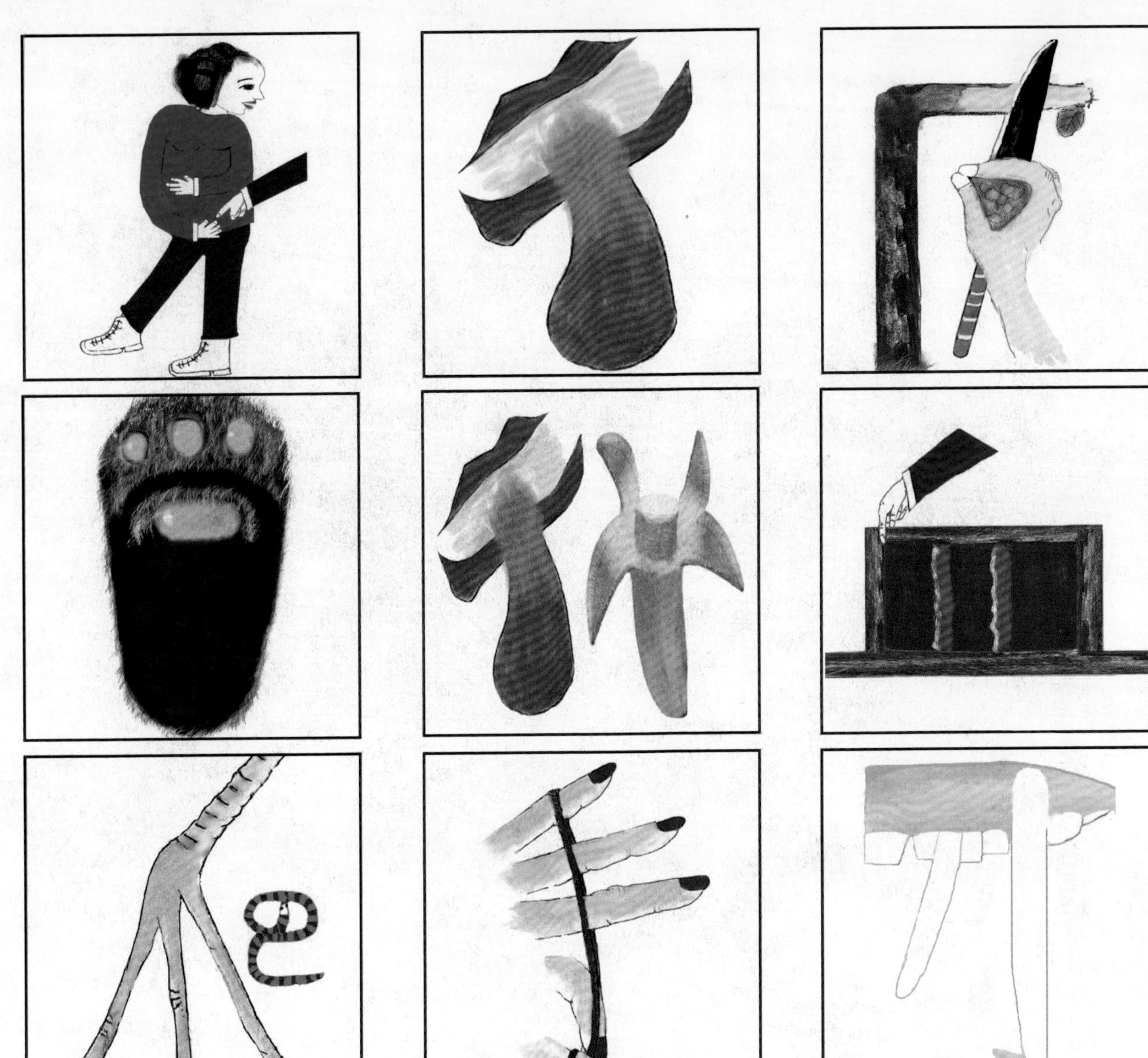

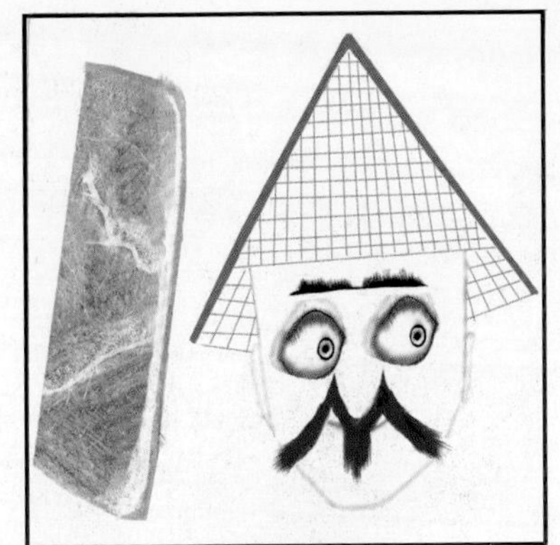
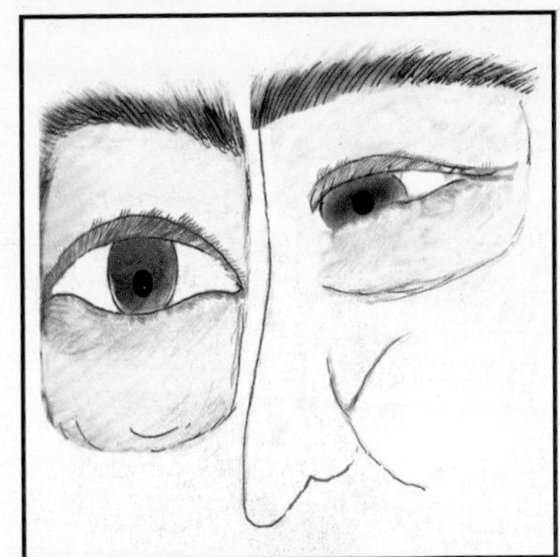
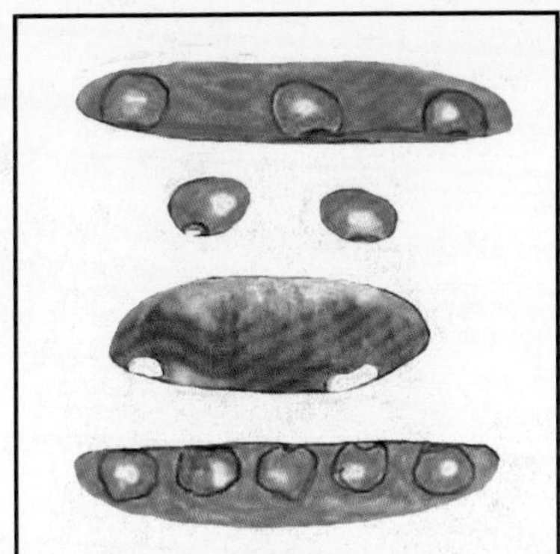

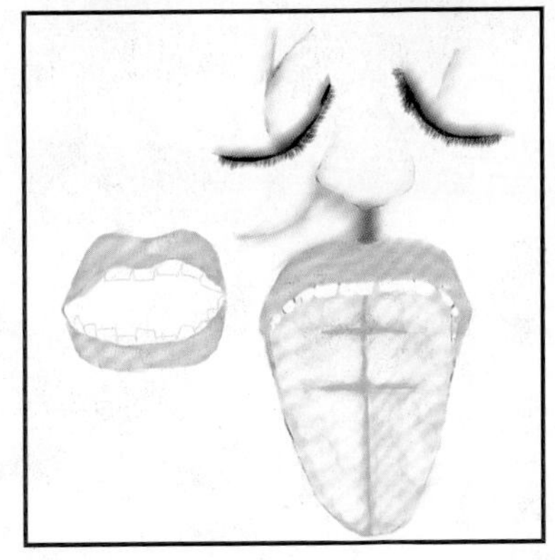
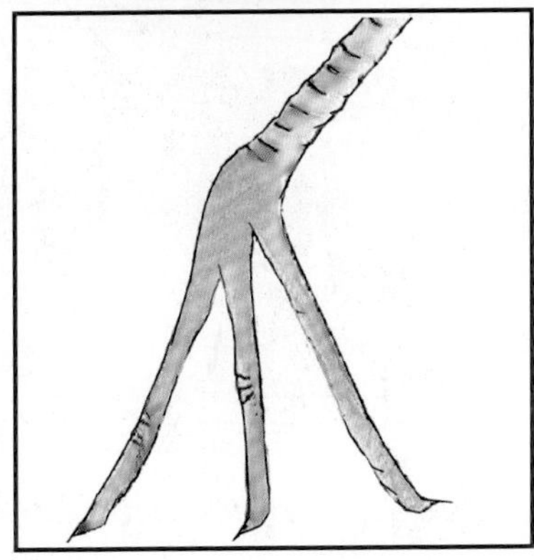

mù 目
目

gǔ 骨
骨

shǒu 手
手

jiǎo 腳
腳

bèi 背
背

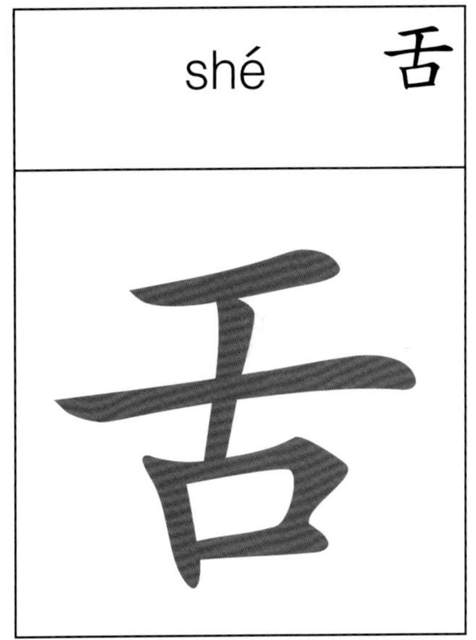
shé 舌
舌

yǎn 眼	yá 牙	chún 唇
眼	牙	唇

zuǐ 嘴	huó 活	jiāo 焦
嘴	活	焦

liǎn 臉	ěr 耳	bí 鼻
臉	耳	鼻

qīng 青	kōng 空	méi 眉
青	空	眉

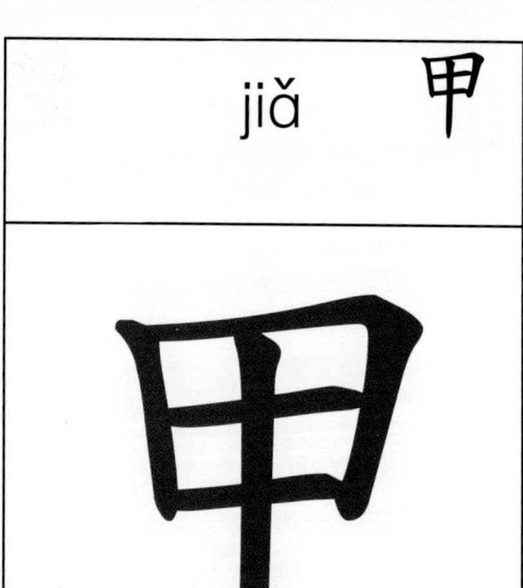

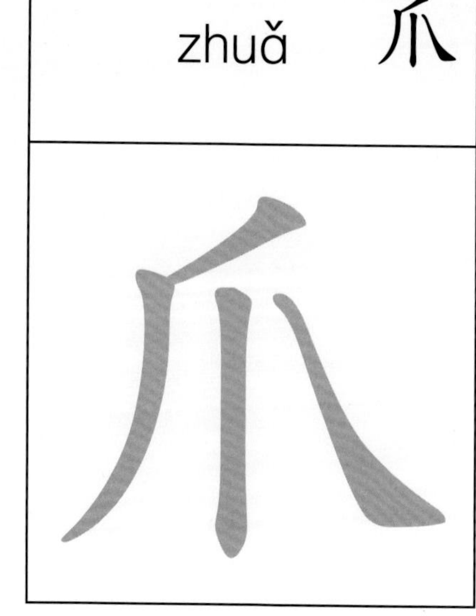

pí 皮

皮

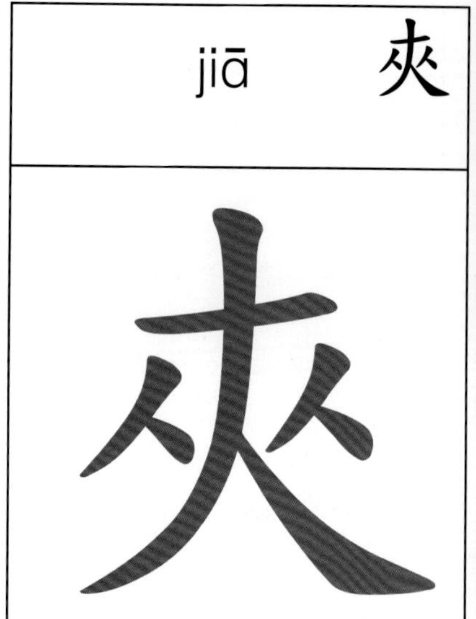

kàn 看

看

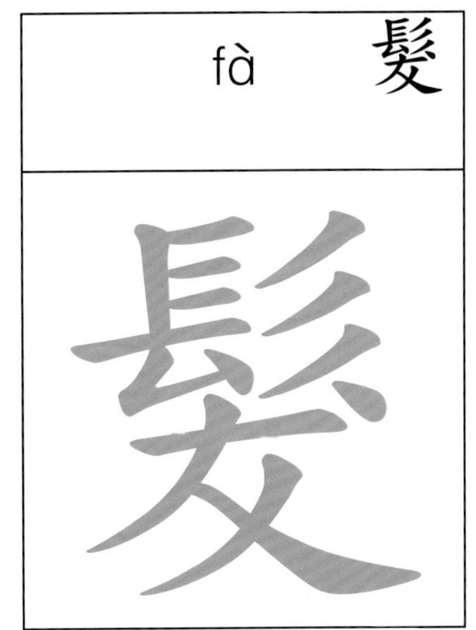

zhǎ 眨

眨

tián 甜

甜

chǐ 齒

齒

xuè 血

pá 爬

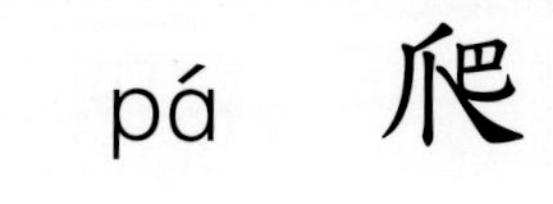

jǐ 脊

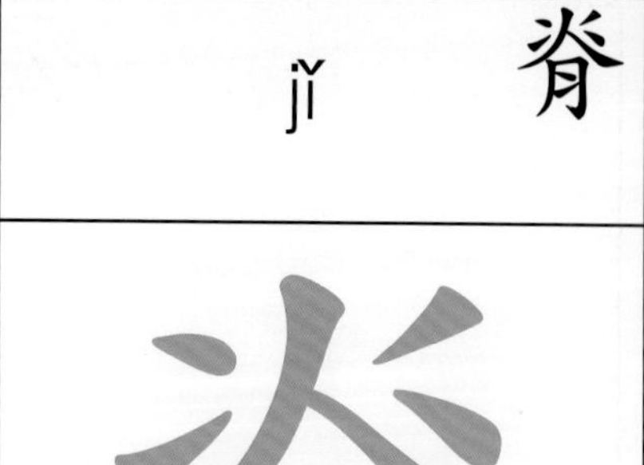

kè 客

máo 毛

gān 甘

yǎo 咬

guā 刮

刮

shēn 身

身

duǒ 朵

朵

yān 咽

咽

guāng 光

光

Vocabulary
詞彙

1. 目 eye
2. 目光 sight/gaze
3. 光 light
4. 燈光 lamplight
5. 相 observe/look
6. 相貌 appearance
7. 眼 eye
8. 眼睛 eye
9. 眨 blink
10. 眨眼 wink
11. 盯 fix one's eyes on
12. 盼 long for
13. 睡 sleep
14. 瞄 set sight on
15. 青 blue/green/black
16. 睛 eyeball
17. 焦 scorch/a surname
18. 瞧 look/glance on
19. 看 look/watch/see
20. 看着 look at
21. 差 mistake/errand
22. 出差 on a business trip
23. 眉 eyebrow
24. 眉毛 brows
25. 毛 hair/wool
26. 汗毛 fine hair on a human body
27. 鼻 nose
28. 鼻子 nose
29. 豆 bean
30. 頭 head
31. 心 heart
32. 思 think
33. 嘴 mouth
34. 嘴巴 mouth
35. 巴 jaw
36. 下巴 jaw
37. 唇 lip
38. 嘴唇 lips
39. 牙 teeth/tooth
40. 犬牙 canine teeth
41. 齒 tooth
42. 牙齒 teeth
43. 空 holllow/empty
44. 腔 chest
45. 力 labour/power
46. 肋 ribs
47. 口腔 mouth cavity
48. 天空 space
49. 肋骨 ribs
50. 胸腔 chest
51. 舌 tongue
52. 舌頭 tongue
53. 甘 sweet/voluntary
54. 甘露 honeydew/banana
55. 甜 sweet
56. 甜蜜 sweet/happy
57. 刮 scrape
58. 刮掉 scrape out
59. 活 alive
60. 生活 life
61. 話 talks/words
62. 恬 tranquil
63. 舔 lick
64. 芽 sprout
65. 客 guest
66. 額 forehead
67. 夾 clip
68. 頰 cheeks
69. 咽 swallow
70. 咽喉 throat
71. 臉 face
72. 臉頰 cheeks
73. 耳 ear
74. 耳朵 ear
75. 朵 quantifier of flowers
76. 花朵 flowers
77. 髮 hair
78. 頭髮 hair
79. 臉面 face/reputation
80. 鼻孔 nostril
81. 額頭 forehead
82. 口水 saliva
83. 手 hand
84. 手指 finger
85. 足 foot
86. 手足 siblings
87. 甲 nail/armor/first
88. 指甲 finger nails
89. 掌 palm/sole/paw
90. 腳掌 sole
91. 腳 feet
92. 腳底 sole
93. 胃 stomach
94. 市 city
95. 肺 lung
96. 胃口 stomach
97. 腸道 intestines
98. 心臟 heart
99. 腎臟 kidney
100. 爪 claw
101. 爪子 claw/paw
102. 爬 climb
103. 爬山 climbing mountain
104. 身 body
105. 身體 body
106. 背 back
107. 後背 back
108. 脊 spine
109. 脊椎 spine
110. 手背 the back of a hand
111. 背後 behind
112. 腳趾 toes
113. 脊骨 a backbone
114. 骨 bone
115. 骨頭 bone
116. 肉 meat
117. 肌肉 muscle
118. 皮 skin
119. 樹皮 bark
120. 血 blood
121. 血管 blood vessel
122. 咬 bite
123. 咬人 biting
124. 骨肉 relatives
125. 皮毛 fur
126. 血液 blood
127. 手腕 wrist
128. 肩膀 shoulder
129. 大腿 thigh
130. 胳膊 arm
131. 脖子 neck